HIS KNIGHT

CHARITY PARKERSON

His Knight

By

Charity Parkerson

--Warning: This book is intended for readers over the age of 18.

Editor: Hercules and Consultants
Photographer: Michel Prince | Royal Touch Photography

❋ Created with Vellum

INTRODUCTION_
TRAGEDY BROUGHT THEM TOGETHER.
LOVE WILL FORGE THEM LIKE STEEL.

The last thing Benny expected was to find himself in the middle of an active shooter event on campus. Canyondale University isn't the type of place he imagined becoming the center of such brutality. After getting shot in the thigh, he would've been dead if not for the SWAT member who rushed to his aid at the moment one of the gunmen was bent on finishing the job.

An explosion of violence is a typical day for Wyatt. It's his job to charge headfirst into the worst situations. This time is different. Downed by several bullets and left for dead, he might not have made it out alive if not for an unlikely hero—a young college student named Benny. Now, Wyatt can't stay away from Benny. The man's dry wit and courageous heart has him mesmerized. Unfortunately, Wyatt's near-death experience has his ex seeing the light and wanting him back.

Relationships built under such stressful circumstances aren't known to last, especially when meddling exes are involved. Thankfully for Wyatt, Benny isn't easily budged, and he's not giving up his knight without a fight.

CHAPTER ONE_

THE COPPERY SCENT OF BLOOD BAKING ON THE
hot cement mixed with the smell of oil from the stain
beneath Benny's head. The Arizona sun had been
relentlessly beating down on the pavement long
before Benny had been forced to hug it. His skin
fried just like an egg from one those educational
videos about not leaving your pets in cars. He swore
he could smell his flesh cooking. His fear overcame
the discomfort, even as it heightened all his senses. It
was eerily quiet on the Canyondale campus, except
for the occasional pop of gunfire in the distance.

   People say hindsight is twenty-twenty. In
Benny's case, it was more like thirty-forty. Of course,
it was possible that was the blood loss making his
brain glitch. The weirdest shit always happened to
Benny. In this instance, it was the most horrific shit,

but there was that one time a custodian had tried cleaning the urinal while Benny was using it. Once, he'd been mistaken for one of the royal princes. The youngest, he thought, but he could barely understand the girl through her screaming and crying. He'd faked a British accent, signed some shit, and then he'd done what he always did—posted the story on his blog. The funniest part of the entire situation was that Benny was Korean, and the prince was a ginger, but if a person couldn't laugh at themselves...

Today wasn't that day. As he hid under the front end of a SWAT truck, bleeding on the pavement and holding the hand of a downed policeman, Benny went over the day's events in his head. If he lived, this was definitely going on his blog. He tried searching for anything funny to share with his readers—a silver lining. By nature, he was a happy person. He loved making other people laugh. Thinking about anything at all was better than the alternative—like how this cop who'd saved him was about to die while Benny watched. The man's light green eyes dimmed by the second.

"What's your name?" Benny whispered. He had to know. He didn't want to die with a stranger.

"Wyatt," the man whispered back.

There it was—a silver lining. He'd been Wild West style saved by a cop named Wyatt. Even though it hurt like his insides were being ripped to shreds, Benny moved closer to the man. "I'm Benny."

Wyatt smiled. It was faint, but Benny didn't miss it. "Stay still, Benny. They're coming back our way."

At Wyatt's warning, the terror sank its claws in once more. He clenched his teeth to keep them from chattering. Wyatt's eyes were the only thing keeping him sane. He wondered if he'd look back on this day and hate his nine-a.m. college professor for sending him outside into a hail of gunfire because that was the way his stupid brain worked. Benny's mind always latched on to the ridiculous details, even when in danger of dying bloody, it seemed. He would still be sitting in class half-awake right now if Professor Thomalson didn't have a thing for him. He should've confessed he was gay and let her down easy a long time ago, but she was eighty if she was a day, and he liked being teacher's pet. She'd forgotten her bag in her car. That was it. The turning point in his day. She'd handed Benny her keys, given him directions to her car, and like that, he'd been free to walk the campus, getting credit for class without the bullshit work.

They'd locked the campus down the second her

car had come into view. He'd looked down at his phone when the piercing alarm had come in. Seconds later, the world exploded. There had to be at least five shooters. All in full riot gear with automatic weapons. Wasn't this high school shit? Who shot up a college campus? Yeah, he'd heard of the occasional random crazy dude with a handgun or knife, but fucking automated weapons. The world was insane.

He'd already been down, shot in the thigh, when the SWAT truck rolled up. Benny hadn't seen it coming. All he'd seen was the gun pointed at him and his life flashing before his eyes. He should've gone for that threesome his ex David had offered. Sure, he would've hated himself afterward, but that was mostly true already anyway.

Gravel crunched nearby, pulling Benny from his scattered fucked-up thoughts. Wyatt's gaze screamed for Benny to stay quiet. The footsteps slowed near Benny's head. He couldn't look. Hell, he couldn't breathe. Benny was convinced his heartbeat and rapid breaths could be heard around the world. He considered covering his mouth to stifle the noise, but he was too scared. His body was on lockdown.

"Driver's side door is locked."

"Passenger side too."

Fuck. There were two of them.

"Goddamn pigs. Search their pockets for the keys."

Wyatt scrambled to push a set of keys Benny's way before closing his eyes and falling still. Benny moved slow, closing his fingers around the set of keys. Black military style boots appeared at the front of the truck, pulling Wyatt away and flipping him over. Benny didn't blink as he watched the man searching Wyatt's pockets. He expected the guy would turn his head at any second and see him. Benny couldn't decide who he feared for the most—himself or Wyatt. The dude moved to the next body and searched.

"Nothing. One of the other three who got away must've had the keys. Fuckers," he spat, kicking the dead cop. Benny jumped as he shot the man again.

"Quit wasting ammo," the other one called. Goddamn. He was still right there. Feet from Benny's head. Still, he couldn't take his eyes off Wyatt, searching for any signs of life. Either the man was damn good at playing dead or he'd passed when the guy moved him. There was so much blood. No way could one person lose that much and live.

"Motherfuckers. I guess we'd better go hunt down the other three if we want this truck. If I'm dying here today, all these bastards are burning with me."

Benny listened to the whole thing on the edge of hyperventilating. He didn't want to burn today. Graduation was three weeks away. He didn't have any family. What would happen to his body? Jesus, who would clear his browser history? The keys he held cut into his hand, dragging him back to reality. He wondered how much of the blood coating the pavement was his. Everything was getting hazy—like looking at the world through a dirty window. Of course, the fact that he'd been holding his breath, expecting to get caught and killed for the past five minutes didn't help matters.

Two sets of boots moved away. Benny took one breath and then another. The moment the men disappeared from sight, Benny gingerly wormed his way out from beneath the truck. He moved slowly, because it hurt, and there was at least one more shooter out there. The other two lay dead between Wyatt and the other cop. When he didn't see anyone, and no shots rang out, Benny hobbled over to Wyatt. He didn't move when Benny touched him, but he had a pulse. Hobbling back to the truck, he quickly unlocked the doors and opened the back. Moving as fast as possible and with adrenaline on his side, Benny dragged Wyatt into the back. The moment he slammed the door closed, he knew he'd fucked up. That shit was loud as hell in the otherwise empty lot. The first black-clad figure appeared from around the corner. Only the truck separated him from death. The man raised his gun, and Benny dove behind the wheel. The bullets struck, making Benny's heart stop before he realized the car was obviously made of sterner stuff. His hands shook as he shoved the keys in the ignition. Two men rushed the truck. The vehicle fired to life and Benny jerked it into gear and slammed his foot on the gas, clipping one of the men who wasn't quick enough to get out of the way. He didn't look back. Survival was all he cared about. At the edge of campus, he could see the barricade in the distance. Flashing lights blocked every exit.

The radio buzzed, snagging Benny's attention. He snatched up the handset without a plan in place and hit the button. "This is Benjamin Lee. Please don't shoot me. I'm already having a really shitty day."

A deep rumble of laughter came from the back, bringing a wave of relief. Holy fuck. They might really live through this after all.

CHAPTER TWO

Pain warred with oblivion. Wyatt couldn't decide which was worse. The images living in his mind would haunt him forever if he lived past today. Steve and Mark were dead. That much he knew. He'd seen them go down moments before the first bullet tore through his arm. They'd worked together for five years. Both men were married with kids. Steve's wife was pregnant with their fifth daughter— due any day. That little girl would never know how amazing her dad had been. Wyatt's throat burned. He no longer knew if it was from physical or mental pain. Each time he regained consciousness, he begged for information that no one would give him. That didn't stop him from trying. Wyatt didn't like being ignored.

"Where's the kid who saved me? Did he make

it?" Wyatt had to know. That kid had saved his life. Wyatt had been there, and he still didn't know how the kid had pulled it off.

"Sir, I need you to be still."

"What about the rest of my team? Did they make it out?" Nothing. People scrambled around him, tugging at his clothes and pressing on things that made him scream. "I need to know about the boy. He was in bad shape. I think he used up what blood he had left, dragging me out of there."

"We need another bag of O positive over here."

Goddamn it. It was like he was already dead. No one was listening to him. What had the kid said his name was? Wyatt searched his too-low-on-oxygen brain. *Benny*. "Where's Benny?" Wyatt roared, finally drawing gazes his way.

A brunette with dark eyes met his stare. "Officer Knight, I promise I'll answer all your questions the moment you're stable. Right now, I'm trying to save your life. Please let us work." Her words did nothing to calm him or reassure him. With the last of his energy, Wyatt slammed his head against the gurney. He didn't want to die for no reason. If Benny hadn't made it, then it was all for nothing. The woman squeezed his shoulder and leaned close to his ear. "The young man you came in with is being prepped for surgery. Don't worry. He's stable. Just let us help you, and I'll make sure you see each other soon."

Wyatt gave her a short nod and closed his eyes. That was good. Whatever happened now would happen. It was not like he'd ever expected to live this long.

"I'M GOING to lift up your gown and take a look at your thigh."

Benny tried holding the material down. "What is it with women hitting on me today? Look, I'm gay." Benny swiped his hand over his face. "Sheesh, if I'd said that like nine months ago to Professor Thomalson, I wouldn't be in this mess."

The brunette with dark eyes looked a step beyond stunned. That thought brought Benny up short. What was a step beyond shocked? Surely there was a definition or something somewhere. "Whoa. You're really high right now."

"My head is definitely swimming," Benny admitted at her observation.

"Close your eyes and relax. I'm going to take a look at your wounds."

Benny tried sitting up again. "Damn, you're gonna go poking at my wounds without numbing anything?"

He wasn't sure, but Benny thought she might be suppressing an eye roll. "You're on painkillers," she reminded him.

Benny didn't bother hiding his eye roll. "Painkillers don't do anything for the pain. They just make you high. I should know because I'm the one who's high."

A small smile hovered on her lips. "Are you in pain?"

Benny thought it over. "No."

"Then the painkillers are doing their job, because you have a couple of gaping holes in your thigh."

"Jesus," Benny breathed. "You still haven't fixed that?"

"I'm not a surgeon," she said, sounding calm. "I'm your doctor. Dr. Kidd," she reminded him. "Now, seriously, just close your eyes. They'll be taking you down to surgery soon enough."

"What about Wyatt?" Benny asked, ignoring her order and fighting against the spinning room.

"Who's Wyatt?"

"The cop. He saved me. Is he alive?"

She dropped her gaze to his thigh and inspected his wound. "I'm not allowed to give out patient info. That's against privacy laws."

Benny scrambled to sit up. "Then I'll go find him myself. He can't die. Obviously, someone needs to do something."

"Jesus," the doctor muttered under her breath while forcing him back down. "Look, are you a doctor?"

Her question was so ridiculous, it gave Benny pause. "No."

"Then what will you do for him that we can't?"

Fuck, he hated that she made sense. "For one thing, if he's dead, I plan to kick his ass back to life."

"With one leg?" she deadpanned.

Benny thought it over, remembering Wyatt's eyes. They were too beautiful to no longer exist. He couldn't accept that fate. Benny gave her a short nod. "Yes. With one leg."

She swiped her hand over her face. "Okay, listen. Just relax and get your leg fixed. When you're awake and can be moved, I'll find you a wheelchair and I'll take you to see him."

A smile exploded across Benny's face. "So he is alive."

"I did not give you patient info," Dr. Kidd said,

sounding stern. "For all you know, I could be wheeling you down to the morgue, but I'm not," she added.

Even through a haze of high, Benny recognized she might be only placating him. "You'd better not be just trying to keep me calm. I'll yell up and down these halls until someone takes me to him."

She sighed. "I swear, even if I'm off the clock, I'll keep my word."

Benny finally closed his eyes, giving in to the meds. His smile didn't abate. "I think you like me a little."

Dr. Kidd chuckled. "I get the feeling you've never met a soul without leaving an impression."

"Don't be hitting on me," Benny said, feeling the world slipping away. "I've already had a lot happen today."

BETWEEN THE ANESTHESIA from his surgery and the massive painkillers, Wyatt was in and out. Each time he'd awoken, he'd been alone except for the occasional nurse. He tried asking after Benny, but either they ignored him or the meds pulled him under again before he heard the answer. He jerked awake as the door to his hospital room opened, slamming back against the wall. A nurse steered another bed inside the room. He bit back a groan. Being stuck in the hospital sucked bad enough without having to share a room. Fucking shitty insurance. His inner cursing died away as he caught sight of Benny. He tried sitting up. His attempts died on a gasp. Dr. Kidd followed Benny's bed into the room.

She shook her head when she spotted Wyatt trying to sit up. "I thought you'd be happy to see him, and I did promise the both of you I'd let you see each other. Plus, hospital bills are cheaper this way."

Wyatt's gaze never left Benny. He wasn't moving.

"I hope this is okay," Dr. Kidd added.

"It's fine," he muttered absently. "Is he okay? He's not moving."

She patted his shoulder. "He's fine. It's the anesthesia. He'll be out of it for a while. But I spoke to him when he came to for a few minutes in recovery. I let him know you'll be sharing a room, since he was adamant about checking on you." She laughed. "A heroic trait you both share, it seems. Anyhow, I also got his permission to share his medical information with you. I worried you might terrorize the nurses if I didn't."

Wyatt rolled his eyes. "I'm not that bad."

Dr. Kidd crossed her arms over her chest. Her eyebrows rose. "Okay, then tell me what you'd do if I told you right now I can't update you on his condition due to privacy laws?"

Maybe she had a point. "I'd terrorize the nurses," Wyatt admitted with a smile.

"Yep," she said, looking triumphant. "Luckily, Benny was fine with me updating you. His upper thigh is a mess. There were two entry wounds and only one exit wound, so we had to do a full body scan to find the other bullet. It turns out there were three bullets still in his leg. The best we can figure was with the automatic fire, the entry points were so close together, and the wounds such a mess, we couldn't tell how many times he'd actually been shot. It looks like at least one of the bullets bounced off his bone and tore up as much stuff as possible before finally stopping near his hip. It took several hours of repair. He lost a lot more blood than anyone realized and they lost him once on the table." Wyatt's heart stopped before racing up again. Dr. Kidd kept talking like she hadn't punched him in the gut. "He's stable now, and he'll be fine. Unfortunately, he won't be using that leg anytime soon. In truth, he's lucky he got to keep it. Like you, it'll be awhile before he goes home, so you'll make perfect roomies." She pulled a face before adding, "And maybe this way, we can keep the two of you from tearing down the building trying to check on each other."

"He is the stubborn type," Wyatt said, making the doctor roll her eyes.

"You two will be the best of friends after this. I can already see it. Let him get some sleep," she fussed. "You can pester him over his health when he wakes up. Plus, you should be sleeping too."

"Okay," Wyatt said, willing to give a little now that she'd arranged a way for him to keep an eye on Benny. He eyed the man next to him. Jesus, he looked like a freaking angel, even pale from blood loss. Funny how those angelic looks had turned into a warrior's under the worst of circumstances. "Would you leave that open?" Wyatt said, panicking when the nurse tried pulling the curtain closed. She eyed him, looking confused. "Please?" he added. "I need to know he's okay."

She eyed Dr. Kidd. The doctor sighed. "You may as well leave it open. If not, this one is likely to climb from the bed to do it himself when we leave." With a short nod, the nurse left the curtain open between them before heading for the door with Dr. Kidd on her heels. "Get some sleep," she said, sounding like his mom, before pulling the door closed behind her.

Wyatt stared at Benny's still form. "Benny," Wyatt said, keeping his voice low in case the man was sleeping. He really did plan to keep his word to Dr. Kidd if Benny was asleep.

"I'm surprised you remember my name," Benny said, sounding like he'd been chewing on glass. "How are you doing?"

Like Wyatt would ever forget Benny's name. "Looks like I took about eight bullets in different places."

Benny hissed.

Wyatt rushed to reassure him. "Most of them are superficial. My gear definitely gave you time to save me. The worst shot I took was to the back. It grazed my kidney, so they're watching it and hoping I don't lose it."

"Goddamn," Benny said, sounding half asleep.

A shot of fear ran through Wyatt. He hadn't said any of the things he needed to say to Benny. The words rushed from his lips. "Thank you for not leaving me behind." He balled his hands into fists to keep his hands from shaking as he said the words. If one of them didn't make it through the night, Wyatt needed Benny to know he owed him everything.

"What's your last name?" Benny asked, ignoring Wyatt's gratitude.

Wyatt smiled into the darkened room. He was a prideful person. He didn't thank people often, but this was huge. It seemed Benny wasn't one to take praise well. Wyatt got it. "It's Knight. What's yours?"

"You're fucking with me, right?" Benny said, his voice heavy with laughter. "I got saved by a cop named Wyatt Knight. That's awesome." His low chuckle had Wyatt's cheeks aching.

"It's inherited. I'm a junior. You never answered me."

"It's Lee. My mom loves all things America. She named me the most American thing she could think of—Benjamin Franklin Lee." It was Wyatt's turn to laugh. Pain shot through his chest and it turned into a cough. Benny tried reaching for the remote to the bed without luck. "Do I need to call the nurse? Are you okay?"

After a few deep breaths, Wyatt managed to control the spasms. "I'm good. Well, good might be a stretch, but I'm still kicking."

"You saved me first," Benny said, rapidly changing the subject. "I just need to say that before I pass out again. You were amazing and heroic. No way could I have left you out there, even if meant we might die together."

It turned out that Wyatt wasn't much on praise either. "Is it okay if we leave the curtain open?"

Wyatt saw the flash of Benny's smile in the otherwise dim room. "I'd like that."

It was possible Dr. Kidd might've made the most dead-on prediction ever. Wyatt was certain Benny would be his friend for life.

CHAPTER THREE

THEY NEVER TURNED ON THE TV. FOR A FULL week, they slept and talked. The funny thing was, it was never about anything heavy. Benny knew Wyatt's shoe size and that he had a sister deployed overseas. He'd even met the man's mom. Benny told Wyatt about his blog and the time he'd gotten stung by a jellyfish. Wyatt had laughed until he'd fallen into a coughing fit over Benny's description of the three old grandmas who'd offered to pee on his arm to make the sting go away. Benny had tried to stop, but he couldn't. Wyatt's laugh was amazing. He'd pushed his luck and Wyatt's health by telling how one of the old ladies had confessed she might make it worse since it burned when she peed.

While Wyatt slept, Benny shamelessly watched. Two nurses had come and gone, checking in. No one tried closing the curtain between them any longer. They would be going home soon. It was bittersweet. Benny was ashamed to admit, he was kind of scared to go home. Not only would he have to find a way to survive with no help, Wyatt wouldn't be there at night when the flashbacks came. At the oddest of times, Benny's teeth would chatter. He'd been forced to lock his jaw too many times to count, out of the blue and for no reason at all. He understood PTSD like he never had before. There was no logic to it. All five shooters had been killed on the scene. When several of Wyatt's cop buddies had come and gone over the past week, Benny had shamelessly eavesdropped as they kept Wyatt updated. Two members of his team were dead. Their funerals had passed without Wyatt in attendance. That had been a dark day—one where Wyatt had barely spoken. Benny hadn't either since he had a bad habit of cracking jokes under pressure.

In total, thirty-seven people had lost their lives, either that day or succumbing to their injuries afterward. All five shooters, two cops, six faculty members, twenty-two students, plus the father and mother of two of the shooters who were brothers—all dead pointlessly. The entire situation was fucked up and would go down in history as the country's deadliest school shooting. All because some fraternity had been banned for a year for an ugly hazing incident. Crazy people always found each other. Benny didn't know how. He couldn't even find one person to go to the movies with and these five people found one another to go on a killing spree. Life was funny. Popularity was wasted on the popular.

Wyatt's friends burst in, startling Wyatt awake. Benny winced at Wyatt's pained expression—like he'd jerked his stitches by moving too fast. Wyatt's friend, Darrel, led the pack. From what Benny understood, he was the only one who worked directly with Wyatt, even though they all worked in some form of emergency services. Darrel's jet-black hair and light brown eyes combined with a nice body, made him a good-looking guy. The way he carried himself—as if he knew exactly how he looked —took a few points away in Benny's book. Benny only knew the man's name from his eavesdropping. Usually, when Wyatt's friends came to visit, Benny pretended to be asleep. Sometimes being an introvert sucked, but they were too big and took up too much space in the room. Benny didn't want to spend an hour tugging at his clothes, rearranging his covers, and brushing his fingers through his hair while trying to anticipate which part of him they'd judge first. His brain was fucked up like that. The second man through the door was Richie. He was the blond of the bunch. The man's expression was off putting. He always had a deep line between his eyes as if trying to work out some horrible thing inside his head. Benny thought he was some sort of DEA officer, but he couldn't be sure. Jayden brought up the rear. If Benny had to guess, he'd say Jayden was the youngest. He was also the quietest, so Benny knew next to nothing about the skinny brown-haired guy other than he was an EMT.

Darrel was the loudest and Benny wasn't surprised when he came in as noisily as possible. "Shit, man. You look like hell. Would you believe we ran into Kayla outside?"

"Shut the fuck up," Wyatt said, raising the head of his bed. Damn, Benny really wanted to know who Kayla was.

"Yeah. Jayden reminded her you still have a restraining order against her ass and offered to walk her out. Since she didn't feel like going to jail tonight, she went on her own."

"Your ex-wife is crazy for real," Jayden said, jumping in.

So Wyatt had a crazy ex-wife. He'd figured

Wyatt was straight. It seemed like Benny never felt an ounce of attraction to anyone unless they were out of his reach. That didn't explain the lump rising in his throat. Things were better this way. Really, they were.

Wyatt's gaze slid Benny's way. For a moment, Benny swore the man looked almost guilty. When he realized Benny wasn't pretending to sleep this time, he motioned toward the men who'd burst into their room. "If these guys get on your nerves, just let me know, and I'll clear them out."

Benny's worst fears came to life. All heads turned his way. He tugged at his hospital gown and blushed. Yep. He should've faked his death. There was nothing he hated more than being the center of attention. It would be a long damn night.

THE INSTANT WYATT called attention to Benny, he regretted it. He wasn't sure if it was due to Benny's blush, which was adorable, or the way Darrel stared at the man with interest.

Darrel eyed Benny from head to toe as he spoke. "I forgot you were sharing a room. Hey, dude, it's you," Darrel said, snapping his fingers when he obviously recognized Benny from the news.

Benny looked like a deer caught in the headlights. "Yeah. Every day of the week." Wyatt thought he might've added "unfortunately" to the end, but his mumbling made it hard to tell.

"No," Darrel said, waving a dismissive hand. "You're the kid from the van. The one who saved Wyatt. Dude, that was badass."

Benny's blush deepened.

Wyatt couldn't look away. "Look, guys, I think we're probably keeping Benny from getting the rest he needs."

Darrel motioned toward the curtain. "You want me to shut this?"

Wyatt got the impression he asked the room in general. Benny answered first. "Please don't. It feels like I'm shut away in the corner when that thing is closed. You're not bothering me. Dr. Kidd found a charger for my phone, so I'll probably toss in my headphones and get some work done."

It was obvious Darrel was interested. A little too interested. "What kind of work do you do?"

"Besides being a full-time student, I do social media marketing for a major global retailer. That's my major—marketing."

Before Wyatt realized what was happening, Darrel had moved closer, along with the rest of the group. Darrel claimed the chair on Benny's side of the room.

"You're not the person responsible for all those ads that pop up on my accounts, are you?"

Wyatt watched the migration while barely listening to the conversation. He didn't want Benny to feel uncomfortable. His eyes stayed locked on Benny, checking for any sign the man was bothered by the attention. Benny's smile was infectious. When he spoke, he moved his hands as if his voice wasn't engaging enough to hold everyone's attention. It hadn't escaped Wyatt's notice that no one other than hospital staff had come to visit Benny the whole time they'd been there. Pride for the awesome friends he'd made over the years rose in Wyatt's chest. They were good men, taking care of a man who'd earned their respect through sacrifice. Benny's words from their first together night rang through Wyatt's mind. *No way could I have left you out there, even if it meant we had to die together.* Wyatt's throat tightened. He trusted his friends. They all knew what it was like to work under the worst conditions and they'd die for one another. Steve and Mark had already given their lives. He hadn't processed that yet, but this guy, he'd been a stranger to Wyatt. Not only that, but a young college kid. He didn't owe Wyatt anything. When Wyatt had jumped from the vehicle, into gunfire, he'd done his job. He'd dragged Benny to the front of the truck and ordered him to crawl underneath. It hadn't been a heroic move. In truth, it had been his training setting in. Logic. The vehicle was armored. Benny was an unarmed civilian whose presence was a distraction. The faster he'd gotten the man to safety, the quicker he'd been able to focus on the problem. Then, he'd gotten shot. Everything from that point had rested on Benny's courage.

The need to do something or say something made him insane. He'd thought several times that surely there was some action or speech that would make them even. But nothing powerful enough ever came to him, so he watched Benny and hoped for a sign. "I saw Dr. Kidd chatting with you earlier. Did she say when you're getting sprung?" Wyatt asked over the top of the noise.

Benny smiled, looking grateful for the interruption. "It's looking like it'll be tomorrow."

"Hey, me too." That was great news. He didn't want to stay past his release, but he would, so Benny wouldn't be alone. This was better.

Darrel stood. "We should celebrate. Surely you're sick of this hospital food by now. The boys and I could go grab some pizza and whatnot. What do think?"

Wyatt thought Darrel kept looking at Benny like he'd be the man's next meal, but Benny looked thrilled at the possibility of eating anything other than bland baked chicken, so he agreed. "Sure. Let's do it. I'll throw in twenty bucks if you'll grab a twelve-pack of soda. I know they're looking out for my bruised kidney by only giving me water, but I'd kill for some caffeine."

"Me too," Benny said, winning points all over the place. "I'd be more than happy to kick in some money."

Darrel winked at Benny. "I've got you covered."

Benny blushed again and dropped his gaze to his lap while he readjusted his covers for the tenth time. While everyone dug out their wallets and money changed hands, Darrel pulled a card from his wallet and passed it Benny's way. With so much going on around him, Wyatt couldn't hear their conversation. Benny accepted, doubling Wyatt's curiosity. The nosy little kid living inside of him was dancing in place. He wanted to ask. Benny's expression was no help at all. The man was smiling, but he always did.

The second the room cleared, Wyatt couldn't hold his silence. "Sorry about all the commotion. You can't keep these guys reined in."

Benny waved away his concern. "It's fine. Actually, it's kind of nice having company."

Wyatt's nosiness doubled. "Yeah, I've noticed you haven't had a lot of visitors." Or any visitors, but whatever. Wyatt already worried he sounded like a dick. "But I saw Darrel give you his number. You might have more company than you can handle soon." Even though Wyatt's voice was heavy with laughter, he didn't feel it in his heart. He loved Darrel. Honest to god, he really did, but Wyatt would break Darrel's goddamn legs if he moved on Benny.

A line appeared between Benny's eyes. Since he still held the card, Wyatt didn't see how Benny could deny it, but he looked confused. He flashed the card Wyatt's way. "He gave me the number to some sort of victim support line."

"Um, yeah." He knew Darrel better than that. "You might want to check the back."

Benny eyed the card, flipping it over. "Oh. Ha. Darrel Johnson 555-8989."

A wave of jealousy overcame Wyatt. In a detached sort of way, Wyatt had noticed before now how hot Benny was. He was obviously of some Asian descent, but mixed. His skin and hair were both dark, but his eyes were blue. He was a combination Wyatt had never seen before. Even with his hair a mess, standing in every direction, the guy was hot as hell, but it wasn't comfortable. Benny was obviously young. Much too young for Darrel and him.

Fuck it. He had to know. "How old are you?"

Benny looked up from the card and met Wyatt's gaze. "Twenty-two."

Jesus, he was barely old enough to drink. He was definitely too young for the impure thoughts he gave men. Wyatt tried playing off his question as unrelated to dating Darrel. "I guess you're pretty close to graduating."

Benny nodded, but he looked sad. "I was supposed to graduate in two weeks, but I don't know if they're pushing things back or what. Not to mention, I don't know how I'll get there or get across the stage. Things are sort of fucked up now."

Wyatt's mind was doing all sorts of things he tried hiding from his expression. To hear Benny talk, when he left here, there would be no one at all. "Program my number into your phone," Wyatt said, wondering why he hadn't done so before now. "When you find out about graduation, let me know.

I'll make sure you get there and across the stage. You shouldn't get screwed out of that." Benny's smile made Wyatt's offer worthwhile. Benny might be too young to date, but they were friends. Wyatt wasn't giving that up.

———

Even though Wyatt had—technically— been released already, and his mom was there to drive him home, Wyatt dragged his feet. Benny was still in the process of getting sprung and Wyatt didn't want to leave until he knew for certain Benny would be okay.

"You two came in together, bunked together, and now you're leaving at the same time. It's like you're each other's lucky charms."

Wyatt smiled as he listened to one of the nurses chatting with Benny. The women loved talking to the guy. Of course, Benny was very personable and funny. Unlike Wyatt, who was a bad patient.

Benny signed the clipboard everywhere she instructed as she ran through his after-care instructions. "We also got shot together," Benny said with a chuckle. "That might be enough to cancel out the luck part. We'll see," Benny added, as if this wouldn't be the last they saw of each other. Wyatt's smile wouldn't abate. He was right. The guy had saved his life. Wyatt wouldn't forget him.

The nurse tucked the clipboard beneath her arm and focused on Benny. "Now, you can't drive, so how are you getting home?"

"I'll call a cab."

Wyatt's mom, who'd been equally and shamelessly eavesdropping, perked up at Benny's answer. "You're not calling a cab to take you home from the hospital. Where's your mom?"

Horror crawled over Wyatt, making him realize he'd never get too old to be embarrassed by his mom.

Benny smiled, looking uncomfortable as he answered. "North Korea. She was deported during the big immigration crackdown five years ago. I was born here, so we were separated."

"And your father?" his mom asked, keeping up the third degree while the nurse hung on every word.

"He's American and white, obviously, because look at this awesome mixed skin tone," Benny said, making Wyatt's smile grow. Since he too was the offspring of an interracial couple, he got where Benny was coming from. People loved to ask about his heritage. "But that's the extent of what I know about him," Benny added, making Wyatt want to know everything. "We've never met, and I have no siblings, so it's a cab for me. Don't worry. I'm used to getting by on my own."

Despite Benny's reassurances, Wyatt's mom wasn't having it. He could tell by the set of her jaw. "Is a cabbie going to help you inside with all your stuff?"

The discomfort in Benny's expression notched up. "Um, well, I don't really have stuff, per se. My clothes were lost either to evidence or blood. Dr. Kidd said I could have this hospital gown, and she found me a plastic bag for my phone, wallet, and whatnot."

His mom stood and grabbed Wyatt's overnight bag. Her determined expression made Wyatt proud to call her his mom. There was no way he'd let the man who'd saved his life go home in a hospital gown and in a cab. Fuck, if he had to stay until the pain meds were out of his system just so he could drive Benny home himself, Benny wasn't leaving here like that.

Ella crossed the room with Wyatt's bag in hand. Benny's features closed a little more with her every step in his direction. "No way in hell is someone who saved my son's life leaving here in a hospital gown and in a cab," she said, mimicking Wyatt's thoughts. She grabbed the curtain and yanked it closed, shutting the nurse and herself inside with Benny.

Benny's voice floated through the curtain, sounding muffled and making Wyatt wonder what they were doing to the kid. "He saved my life first, so we're even."

They weren't even. They'd never be even. Wyatt had done his job. Benny had been a fucking hero. There was a huge difference between the two. Maybe Benny wasn't admitting it to himself, because he hadn't really thought about it yet, but he'd been damn close to death. Despite that, he'd somehow dredged up the strength to drag Wyatt into that van and get away from men with automatic weapons. He could've left Wyatt there. No one would've blamed him. A few minutes more and Wyatt would've been dead and no one would've been the wiser. That was not the choice Benny had made, and Wyatt would never, ever forget it.

The curtain reopened and Benny sat, looking shell shocked, wearing a pair of Wyatt's workout shorts and a t-shirt.

"I can't do anything about your bare feet, other than socks, but it'll be fine until you get home. Oh, and we'll run by the pharmacy and get your meds."

"Do you have more women flirting with you?" Dr. Kidd said as she sailed through the door.

"You know the ladies can't resist me," Benny said, blushing and fascinating Wyatt. It was true. They couldn't. Every damn nurse in the building and two women who brought the food stopped by to see the boy as often as they could. But, in this case, it seemed Benny shared some inside joke with the doctor. Damn, the kid really won over everyone he met.

"I came to see if you needed a lift home."

Ella jumped in, reassuring her. "I've got him. Can you believe he'd planned to leave here in a cab?"

"I'm not surprised," Dr. Kidd said, shaking her head.

Wyatt caught Benny's eye and winked. He looked so damn horrified by everyone fussing over him, Wyatt couldn't resist. To his surprise, Benny's blush deepened. All the women fussing over him were older than Benny, but still, the guy should be ecstatic over the attention. Instead, he looked ready to crawl in a hole. If he didn't like people in his space, life was about to get even more uncomfortable. Wyatt didn't doubt for a second the dude's place was crawling with reporters. That thought sucked ass, especially since Wyatt's place probably was too. It didn't matter so much to Wyatt since he would probably go home with his mom for a few days. If Wyatt couldn't do anything else for Benny, maybe he could fix the reporter issue. Wyatt grabbed his phone and started texting people. Just because he was in the hospital didn't mean he was helpless.

OF ALL THE things Benny expected to see when they pulled into the driveway of Benny's duplex, Wyatt's friends and several of his co-workers standing guard wasn't one of them. He wasn't even sure how they knew where he lived. Of course, judging by the huge number of reporters on his lawn, it seemed everyone knew where he lived now. Benny tried hiding his smile as he realized Wyatt's friends were forming a blockade to Benny's door, sparing him from the reporters. Damn, Wyatt was amazing. Benny didn't doubt for a second he'd arranged this greeting. He hadn't considered there might be reporters crawling all over his house. His neighbor—an old man who already hated Benny—was no doubt having a fit and would never forgive Benny for the commotion.

"Look, it's Darrel," Ella said, pointing out where Wyatt's best friend stood near Benny's front door. "Oh, and Jayden. How nice for all your friends to show up," Ella said, sounding as happy as Benny felt. "*Gah*, these reporters. When will they have their pound of flesh? They've already beat this story into the ground. It's past time for them to give the families and victims peace."

"Unfortunately, it probably won't end until everyone has interviewed everyone a hundred times. I appreciate this," Benny said, meeting Wyatt's gaze. "It never occurred to me there would be reporters. I don't know why it didn't, but I'm grateful for the reprieve."

Wyatt winked, making butterflies unexpectedly stir in Benny's gut. No amount of reasoning mattered to his body, it seemed. Even though Wyatt would never see him as more than a friend, Benny hoped he didn't stop coming around. They'd been together twenty-four-seven for the past week. Benny had a terrible feeling his house was about to become a tomb. The solitude he adored seemed emptier than ever before.

CHAPTER FOUR_

It took Benny longer than he'd admit to answer the knocking at his door. His grumbling and cursing died away when he spotted Wyatt on the other side. "Hi." Sheesh, even to his ears, he sounded breathless. He'd always been an idiot.

Wyatt's gorgeous smile made an appearance. "Hi. I figured you were still having trouble getting around by yourself. I've come to help."

Since Benny had been taking care of himself for years, he would've expected pride to make an appearance and use his mouth to shoot Wyatt down. It didn't happen. Benny couldn't stop smiling. He hopped backward so Wyatt could come in. "How is it that you took more bullets than me, but you're up and driving around? I have to anticipate a bathroom break fifteen minutes ahead of time just so I can get there before I piss on myself."

Wyatt's sexy laugh rumbled through the living room. "I don't have crutches hindering me, and I'm used to being in pain. You're young. You haven't gotten there yet."

"I'm not that young." Yeah, even to Benny's ears, he sounded stupid, but he had some pains.

Light green eyes flashed his way. Laughter made them even brighter. "You're young compared to me. I'm thirty-four and I played football through college and two years professionally before tearing out my shoulder. Everything hurts when I get up in the morning. Then some little bastard went and shot me several times." Wyatt shrugged. Benny's mouth watered as he watched the man's massive shoulders lift and roll. "I've just added to the list of shit that pops, creaks, and aches when I crawl out of bed."

Curiosity over that bed ate Benny alive. "I bet it's huge."

Another round of laughter filled the room, feeding Benny's heart. "What?"

"Your bed," Benny clarified, crutching his way back to the couch. "I have no idea why. You just strike me as a man who owns the world's biggest bed."

Wyatt helped him settle back down. "You're such an odd kid."

The words knocked the air from Benny's lungs. Life was unfair. Benny always crushed on the wrong people. It was funny how Wyatt being straight didn't bother him. His type usually was, but the man considering him a child—that was a punch to the gut. Wyatt was right. He was odd.

"Are you okay? Do you need some pain meds?"

Benny shook his head, trying to dispel his black thoughts. It wasn't Wyatt's fault. Benny was always alone, but then again, he wasn't. There was no one in his life directly, but he never sat around the house with his thoughts. "Sorry. I had a weird moment there, feeling sorry for myself," he admitted. Even though he felt stupid for doing so, Benny couldn't stop the confessions. "I've been on my own since I was seventeen. This shit," he said, motioning toward his leg. "It's a new level of bullshit. I'm used to being on the go—classes, library, and volunteering. Sitting here, waiting to heal, is making me nuts."

"That was another worry of mine. You're young."

Fantastic.

"With no parents."

Could this get worse?

"And no one to help you. I thought maybe you could use like a big brother or something."

If Jesus could just take him now, that would be great.

"So I brought some stuff. Hang on," Wyatt said, heading for the door. "I'll be right back." Benny watched Wyatt disappear through the front door. He returned in less than a minute, carrying several bags. His smile wiped away Benny's irritation. "I thought, if you don't mind me hanging around, we could watch some movies, eat some junk, and whatever."

He really wanted to know what "whatever" consisted of, but Benny didn't ask. "You brought food and movies?" Benny couldn't hide the happiness in his voice.

"Yeah, and some other stuff." Wyatt dropped two bags—a plastic bag and what looked to be an overnight bag—on the coffee table. He carried the rest to the kitchen. It killed Benny not being able to follow. Curiosity ate him alive. Wyatt returned empty handed. His gaze landed on Benny. Benny fought not to eat the man alive with his stare. He was fucking perfect. Wyatt wasn't huge. In fact, they were the same height, and Benny was only five-foot-nine, but Wyatt was cut. His shirt molded to every line. His arms made Benny want to cling to them. All

Benny could do was measure each breath and dream. "What would you like to do first?"

At Wyatt's question, Benny wrestled his wayward thoughts to the ground and tried burying them. "I don't know. Your options were vague."

To his surprise, Wyatt crossed the room and pulled him to his feet. Benny wondered if he looked as shocked as he felt as Wyatt held on to him and helped him to the kitchen. Benny lost the battle. His hand landed on Wyatt's stomach. He told himself he braced himself against falling. His body screamed he was a liar. When Benny's fingers collided with Wyatt's abs, he stroked. He didn't mean for it to happen. Wyatt's body made him stupid. The man's skin was soft yet hard. He could feel every muscle rolling beneath the man's skin, but he was like velvet. The second Benny found his hand, sliding across Wyatt's stomach in a loving caress, horror overcame him. He prayed the floor would swallow him. It was like something glitched in his brain, because he did it again, savoring the sensation of silky washboard beneath his palm. He told himself to drop his hand and just hang on to Wyatt's waist. It didn't happen. By the time they made it to the kitchen where Benny could cling to the counter, his humiliation was complete. If Wyatt left him right then, alone with no way back to the couch, it would be what he deserved. The silence between them was deafening. Benny tried several times to force his eyes in Wyatt's direction before succeeding.

When he finally managed to meet Wyatt's gaze, the man looked more thoughtful than annoyed. He turned away, grabbed a stool, and forced Benny to sit before heading for the grocery bags he'd abandoned. Wyatt pulled out a covered glass pan. "I can't take credit for this part. Mom was worried about you too. She sent food. I hope you like lasagna." Benny watched in silence as Wyatt opened every drawer until he found the silverware. He pried the lid from the pan, uncovering a cheese-covered meal. Benny still couldn't make his brain work as he watched Wyatt dig a fork in. "This is Mom's special recipe. If you know women, then you know—whether you like it or not—you should say that you love it." He paused with a fork full of lasagna held over the dish. "Do you have a girlfriend?"

In the worst case of timing ever, Benny's brain fired back to life and a loud burst of horrified-sounding laughter escaped him. He fought for control. Heat crawled up his neck and exploded across his face. Not only had he just felt the man up, now this. "Um, no. I'm gay, which has always seemed like it should be glaringly obvious, but this past year is really teaching me new things." He couldn't stop. The babbling just kept pouring out. "First, Professor Thomalson won't stop flirting and then I get hit on by the chick at the coffee shop. I have three phone numbers from nurses at the hospital, and now, you—"

Wyatt put his hand over Benny's mouth, muffling his words. He fell silent, mostly because he had to snap his teeth together to keep from licking Wyatt's hand. The temptation was real.

"Stop," Wyatt said, looking serious enough that Benny's heart rate slowed. "It was a joke. You're a chick magnet and that cracks me up. Stop explaining yourself. You don't owe it to me or anyone, okay?" He dropped his hand. Benny's throat swelled. Even if he'd wanted to speak, he didn't have the ability. The past week of his life had been hell, but Benny recognized that of all the shit he'd endured in the past seven days, this was the most unfair moment of them all. Wyatt was amazing—like the kind of guy Benny could fall in love with entirely too fast. He'd seen this happen to his friends. Watched them make themselves stupid over a straight guy. Benny never thought it would be him. It seemed life didn't a give fuck what he thought he'd never do.

WYATT HAD to cover Benny's mouth. If he'd let the man ramble a second longer, he would've kissed him, and neither of them needed that. In his profession, he'd heard tons of stories about survivors falling in love under stressful circumstances. It never ended well. He liked Benny. A lot. He was funny and had a dry wit Wyatt had never been able to resist. It was odd for Benny to be so funny, yet be unable to tell when Wyatt was joking. He'd known Benny was gay. First off, a straight dude would've tossed Darrel's number back in his face. Secondly, Benny obviously didn't realize how he looked at Wyatt—like he could eat him alive. Butterflies stirred in Wyatt's gut at the thought. It had been a damn long time since anyone looked at him the way Benny did.

He picked up the fork again and held a bite out for Benny. "Try this."

Benny dutifully opened his mouth and let Wyatt feed him. He chewed. "Holy shit. That's delicious. I can't tell you the last time I had real food. Please tell your mom how much I love her."

Wyatt chuckled. "There's garlic bread and

brownies here too," Wyatt said, deciding to go with pretending nothing happened. "If you want, I'll give you Mom's number so you can thank her yourself."

Benny's face lit. "Is your mom single?"

A surprised snort escaped Wyatt. He couldn't help it. Benny looked so damn earnest. "Yeah, but my dad just passed three months ago. I don't think she's quite ready for you." Wyatt moved to the fridge, where he'd stashed a cold twelve-pack. "I brought beer. If that's not okay, let me know what you'd like to drink, and I'll grab it."

"Beer is fine."

After snagging two beers, Wyatt turned to find Benny stealing another bite. He winked when he noticed Wyatt watching. Wyatt opened the beer and passed it over. Benny took a quick sip. "So, she's not ready for a relationship with a chick magnet. How about another son? Is she adopting?" he asked, looking hopeful.

For a moment, Wyatt couldn't respond. He could never be this man's brother. Wyatt didn't mean for it happen. He set his beer aside and closed the distance between them. "I'm sure she'd love to have you, but then I wouldn't get to do this," Wyatt said, capturing the man's lips.

The instant it registered with Wyatt's brain that

he held Benny's bottom lip between his teeth, he thought to pull away. His body wasn't capable. All because of the sound Benny made the second Wyatt's teeth sank into his flesh. It was the longing of a man too long neglected. Their tongues met. Wyatt took a step closer. Benny gasped in pain, bringing Wyatt back to reality.

He jumped away. "I'm sorry. Jesus." Wyatt swiped his hand over his face, feeling like an idiot. Benny was injured and Wyatt had pawed at him like a fucking idiot. Without looking Benny's way, Wyatt opened the first cabinet door he came to, looking for plates. He moved to the next when he only spotted glasses. The silence of the room sank in. Wyatt finally chanced a glance Benny's way. He looked devastated. It punched Wyatt in the chest.

"You're sorry?"

Wyatt's gaze dropped to Benny's mouth at the question. His stomach cramped with need. "No." His feet carried him across the room before he knew what he'd do. This time, when their lips met, Wyatt knew what to expect. The heat didn't lessen, but he held on to his head. Benny didn't need some huge, horny guy pawing at him while he was hurt. But Benny would heal, and when he did, Wyatt needed him to understand—this was happening. Every sensible idea about relationships formed under pressure had disappeared with the first kiss. This was about more than Benny saving his life. Every night-long conversation through their time in the hospital had led them right here. Benny was giving him a shot. Wyatt was determined the man wouldn't regret it.

Benny was a nibbler. He kept drawing Wyatt's bottom lip between his teeth, biting and then sucking before delving his tongue inside once more. It was damn hard to pull away. Wyatt's cock leaked inside his jeans at the idea of Benny's sexy soft lips wrapped around it. It wouldn't be tonight. Wyatt had to shut things down before horny-man brain took over, turning this into a bad porn movie.

He backed away. Benny's expression almost had him throwing his good intentions to the wind. Flushed cheeks, unfocused gaze, and kiss-swollen lips painted an image Wyatt craved more than oxygen. He couldn't stop himself from brushing his thumb along Benny's bottom lip. "Goddamn," Wyatt breathed before clearing his throat and taking another step back. "Where are your plates?"

Benny absently motioned toward a cabinet behind him. Wyatt set to fixing their food and focusing on his task. He'd always been an idiot, but Benny made him feel downright empty headed.

Wyatt sat braced on the edge of a knife, waiting for the storm as they sat side by side on the couch and ate. Benny did such a damn good job of pretending nothing happened, when he finally broke, Wyatt was almost relieved. Almost.

"You have an ex-wife."

Wyatt should've anticipated Benny would go there first and had some speech prepared. As it was, he didn't know where to start. "Obviously, she was a mistake," he said with a chuckle. Wyatt immediately wished he could take the words back. Not only did he sound like a dick, but Kayla wasn't so bad. She was a little crazy, but it was possible he'd driven her there. There was nothing for it. "I shouldn't have said that. It wasn't fair to her. Actually, all of being married to me wasn't fair. I mean, I never lied to her or anything. She knew I dated mostly men before her, but I'd dated women too. I think she thought our life would be different." Wyatt stopped, because he wanted to explain, but he equally realized Benny probably didn't want to hear any of this.

Benny motioned for him to continue. "Go on.

I'm not bothered," he tacked on, making Wyatt smile. It was like the man could read minds.

"Um, she's a bit of a kink." Damned if Wyatt did feel the blood rushing to his cheeks. He couldn't remember the last time he'd been this uncomfortable.

Rather than laughing at his discomfort, as anyone else would've done, Benny nodded his understanding. "She assumed, since you're bi, you'd be open to having other men join you," Benny said, hitting the nail square on the head.

Relief poured through him. "Exactly. I think she expected life with me would be fun and exciting. In truth, she was alone a lot and worrying over whether I'd live through the night. I tried making her happy. Eventually, I gave in and agreed to let this guy she worked with..." Wyatt wondered again if he told too much.

Benny nodded. "Let me guess, your onetime threesome became their full-time twosome."

"Yes," Wyatt said, sounding every bit as relieved as he felt over not having to spell things out.

"Actually, something somewhat similar happened to my last relationship. Except I refused the threesome, and the twosome continued without me. Funnily enough, when I was hiding under that truck, that's the first thing I thought about when it really hit me I might die. That's kind of depressing," Benny said, sounding sad as he stared at some point over Wyatt's shoulder. Then a hint of a smile touched Benny's lips, and he met Wyatt's gaze. "I also thought there was no way in hell I'd let someone with such beautiful eyes die while I watched."

An odd sensation overcame Wyatt—like he witnessed fate in the making. He shook his head, trying to dispel his random thoughts. "I get the feeling you're an old man trapped in a twenty-two-year-old body." Benny smiled. It turned into a wince as he shifted. Wyatt quickly retrieved the man's empty plate and set it on the coffee table. "You need to stretch out. Here," Wyatt said, patting his lap. "Head here."

Even as Benny rearranged his legs to do as Wyatt bade, he argued. "You're the one who should be stretching out. I still don't get how you're in better shape than me."

The instant Benny's head was in his lap, Wyatt recognized his mistake. He wanted the man there too badly. His fingers immediately sought the man's hair, brushing through his soft locks. "I'm better sitting up. Stretching out pulls at all my wounds. It's awful. I've been sleeping in my recliner because every time I try lying flat, it's like my insides are being shredded. Trust me, you're not alone." He thought it over before adding, "In fact, you're doing me a favor by spending time with me and distracting me from the pain."

"Mhmm," Benny hummed, making Wyatt's dick stir. He'd never heard a man sound more content. "Same. I never have time for pity parties when you're around. It's stupid, but I've almost missed the hospital." It wasn't stupid. Not at all. Wyatt felt the same. He'd been single for a while and was used to the silence. His house had been deafening since leaving his nights with Benny behind. Benny motioned toward the arm of the couch. "If you reach between the cushion and arm, there's a handle there. This side of the couch reclines."

Wyatt found the handle and pulled. "Sweet."

Benny's chuckle vibrated against his crotch. "There's a remote over there somewhere too, if you want to find something to watch. I won't judge you if you fall asleep as long as you don't judge me."

"Go for it. I've missed your snoring."

"Bastard," Benny said, his voice heavy with laughter even as he pinched Wyatt's thigh. Or, rather, he tried a few times to pinch Wyatt without luck. "That's fucked up. Nobody's body should be so goddamn perfect there's no skin to grab."

"Jesus. Go to sleep," Wyatt fussed. In truth, he was flattered and trying to hide it. Wyatt didn't spend a ton of time working out. He was wide framed from playing football and ended up at the gym more out of boredom than any real desire to be there. Now he was happy for all those nights he had nothing better to do. He couldn't stop running his fingers through Benny's hair. It never occurred to him he should find something else to do. He already knew there was nothing on TV that could compete with Benny. The man's breathing deepened. Wyatt knew he should stop touching him and let him sleep. No matter how hard he tried, he couldn't stop, until his eyes grew heavy and every weight he carried slipped away.

WYATT CAME AWAKE WITH A START. For a moment, he stared at the unfamiliar ceiling in confusion. The warm weight in his lap caught his attention. His gaze dropped and collided with gorgeous blue eyes. Damn. Wyatt didn't know how long he'd been sleeping or how long Benny had been watching him.

"I have a problem," Benny said before Wyatt could ask. "My leg is seized up and I can't move."

Although Benny's voice was calm, Wyatt could see the panic in his eyes. In truth, Wyatt wasn't feeling so hot either, which meant he'd been asleep, in the same position with no pain meds, for a long time. "Okay. I got this," Wyatt said, struggling to sit up.

To his surprise, Benny chuckled. "What a fucked up pair we are. I'm thinking the hospital should've kept us a little longer."

Wyatt smiled through the pain of sliding out from underneath Benny. "That's probably my fault. They knew I wouldn't leave if they discharged me alone, and I made a terrible patient."

"I remember," Benny gasped out as Wyatt helped roll him onto his back. "Fuck me," Benny growled through gritted teeth.

Wyatt's body fired to life. It didn't matter Benny's words had been an exclamation of pain. That was the moment Wyatt knew he was in trouble. It was also the moment Wyatt's brain disconnected from his tongue. "If you insist."

Luckily, Benny laughed, obviously assuming Wyatt had been joking. "I'm game. You can only make things better at this point."

Wyatt couldn't contain his smile as his gaze swept Benny's body. He had no idea how to fix him. "Tell me what I need to do."

"Your poor ex-wife. First, you take off your pants."

Despite Benny's laughter, Wyatt could hear the pain behind the words. "Jeez. You're a mess," Wyatt muttered. He went with his gut and gently massaged Benny's leg. Benny released a groan that had Wyatt's cock beating a pattern against the inside of his zipper. "Tell me if I hurt you."

"I'm being serious when I say I don't think you can make it worse."

Wyatt's chest tightened. He couldn't let this man hurt. "Okay. I've got this." He dug through the stuff on the table and found his phone. It seemed there was no line he wouldn't cross for Benny. Wyatt texted Jayden.

Wyatt: *What do I do if a wound stiffens the muscle to the point of excruciating pain?*

Jayden: *Are you okay? Do I need to come over?*

Wyatt: *It's not me. It's Benny. His leg is sort of locked up?*

Jayden: *Make him take all his meds. Alternate heat and ice. Massage around the wound, but be mindful of any stitches. Why are you with Benny?*

Wyatt: *Thank you. He's my friend.*

Jayden: *Oh. Okay. Can I come by when I get off tonight? I need to talk to you about something.*

Wyatt: *Text me when you get off. If I'm home, that's fine.*

Jayden: *Okay.*

Wyatt tossed the phone aside. "Where are your meds? Jayden says you need to take one of everything they gave you."

"Fantastic. I'll be out of it all day. They're in the kitchen."

Wyatt gave him a short nod and stood. "Do you have a heating pad? You need to alternate heat and ice. Also, Jayden says I need to massage around the wound."

"I thought the point was to ease the stiffness. Not make it worse," Benny said, still trying to laugh even though his expression said otherwise.

Wyatt walked backward into the kitchen. "Actually, that's not that bad of an idea. I think I could make you forget about your leg." Wyatt heard himself. He sounded serious and turned on. It was too late to take it back. When Benny's lips parted, and a flush touched his cheeks, Wyatt didn't want to take it back. He turned away before he made things worse. The moment he was out of sight, Wyatt covered his eyes. What the fuck was he doing? For one, he was too old for Benny. Secondly, the man was in pain. Wyatt gathered Benny's meds, a drink, and an ice pack while vowing to do better. He reappeared to find Benny trying to roll off the couch on his own.

"What the fuck are you doing?" The roar was out of his control.

"I gotta pee and you can't help with that," Benny grumbled, still trying to get up.

"For fuck's sake," Wyatt bitched, setting everything on the table. "First, take these meds."

The way Benny downed one of each of the pills said a lot about how bad he had to go. Seeing nothing else for it, he pulled Benny straight up, helping him to his feet. With his weight braced on one leg, Benny made a sound that ripped at Wyatt's throat. The worst part was the way Benny tried to hide it—like he worried Wyatt might think he was dramatic or being weak. No one knew how close Benny had come to losing that leg. He needed help, and he had no one. Fuck that bunch of bullshit. He had Wyatt, and this wasn't happening on his watch.

"Let's speed this up so I can take care of you," Wyatt said, before lifting Benny from his feet and rushing him toward the bathroom.

"Don't," Benny argued, sounding scared. "You'll tear your stitches out."

Wyatt's temper snapped. "Would you stop worrying over me? I know my limitations." He wasn't angry with Benny. Wyatt was pissed off at life for making someone as amazing as Benny have to deal with this mess in the first place, much less alone. He set Benny down inside the bathroom. "I'll wait outside for you. If you need me, yell."

The way Benny blinked at him as he closed the door in his face said a lot about how Benny didn't know what to make of Wyatt. That made two of them. Wyatt didn't know what he was about either. All he knew was—he liked Benny. A lot. Way more than he could shake. A self-deprecating smile tugged at the corners of Wyatt's mouth. Benny made him want to beat his chest and be the strong one—like he needed to prove he was worthy. Wyatt just hadn't decided of what—Benny saving him or Benny keeping him. Maybe it was both.

The water inside the bathroom ran. He could

hear Benny brushing his teeth. Great. Now Wyatt had to pee too. By the time the bathroom door opened, Benny looked halfway human again, albeit a miserable one.

He hopped one step. Wyatt swept him off his feet. Benny had been right. It felt like his stitches were ripping to shreds, but damned if he would show it. He waited until he had Benny settled back on the couch with ice on his leg before running for the bathroom. Benny's laughter followed him down the hall. With his bladder empty and his face washed, Wyatt tried scrubbing his teeth with his finger and some toothpaste before checking his bandages. Everything looked fine. Benny probably didn't weigh enough to do any real damage, but Wyatt hated to ruin his image by having his guts falling out on the floor. By the time he made it back to the living room, Benny had one arm slung over his eyes. Wyatt's heart squeezed in his chest. He got the feeling he wasn't the only one pretending to feel better than he did.

"I'm going to run out to my truck and grab my meds."

"Okay," Benny said without uncovering his face.

Wyatt made it quick. Benny wasn't looking so hot. He popped two pills even though he was only supposed to take one and swallowed them without a drink. Wyatt was back at Benny's side in no time. He pulled the coffee table as close to the couch as he could get and sat before plucking the ice pack from Benny's leg. Wyatt eyed the sweat pants covering his thigh. "Would it be okay if I look at your wound? I'm not a doctor or anything, but it would make me feel better if I could check it over."

Benny's arm lifted enough for his gorgeous eyes to peek out. "I'm supposed to change my bandages anyhow and the meds are kicking in."

Without thought, Wyatt's fingers curled around the waistband of Benny's sweatpants. Benny didn't fight him for the material. Wyatt's cock joined the party the moment he slid Benny's pants down. Benny lifted his hips for Wyatt. Wyatt's mouth went dry. It was exactly the same as if he undressed the man for a different reason. He didn't know how to be clinical about it. Wyatt wanted Benny.

He kept his gaze on his task, trying to hide his lust. Even though Wyatt could've stopped at the knee, he didn't. He peeled Benny's pants off. Since Benny had covered his eyes once more, Wyatt had more freedom than he deserved. He fought to keep his gaze from shifting higher than Benny's thigh.

Instead, he focused on peeling away the surgical tape.

"You'll have to just pull it. There's no good way to get it off," Benny muttered, sounding high.

Wyatt yanked and then winced. He knew that shit hurt. His stomach twisted into knots at the first sight of Benny's thigh. There was no chance Benny would escape horrible scarring. Even still, Wyatt wanted to kiss away the man's pain. He might not have been the one who'd shot him, but Benny had done even more damage saving him. These scars would always be for him.

Still trying to be clinical, Wyatt taped down a fresh bandage. "It looks okay. I think you just need to loosen up the muscle. Maybe tonight, I can set an alarm on my phone for every four hours. We can get up, take our meds, and stretch." Wyatt massaged around Benny's wound as he spoke. "That way, we don't wake up all fucked up again."

"You talk like you're staying again tonight," Benny said around his arm.

"Yes," Wyatt said, rubbing Benny's inner thigh. "I'm making an executive decision here. You're keeping me until you're better. I don't want you being alone and I don't feel as bad when you're around."

Benny peeked out at him again. "What about after I'm better? Do I not get to keep you then?"

Wyatt held his gaze and stroked Benny's leg. "I think we both know you already have me for life." Wyatt just didn't know in what capacity.

While using the outer edge of the bandage as his guide so he wouldn't bump Benny's wounds, Wyatt held Benny's stare as he rubbed his thigh. The man's expression kept him fascinated. Wyatt couldn't lie. Touching Benny like this turned him on, but it was the arousal written on Benny's face that had his dick throbbing. Wyatt couldn't stop. He kept moving higher. It wasn't intentional. He just kept finding his hands moving north. The higher he went, the more the flush of Benny's cheeks deepened. Despite Benny's willingness to chat with anyone who spoke to him, the man's uncomfortable fidgeting around strangers told the real story. Benny was painfully shy. He would never ask Wyatt for anything. Wyatt would never make him. They both knew if Wyatt dropped his gaze, he'd find Benny hard for him. Wyatt wanted to ease Benny's every ache. This time, Wyatt's moves were calculated. He moved higher, intentionally brushing the bulge in Benny's underwear with the edge of his hand. Benny sucked in a ragged breath. Wyatt did again because he needed that sound like he needed oxygen. The third time, he moved slower, dragging out the motion and leaving no room for doubt it had been intentional.

Benny reached down and covered his hand, stopping him. "I should probably put the heating pad on now."

Wyatt didn't move. Benny had shut him down and he wasn't sure what to make of it. It was obvious Benny was aroused, but it was possible he'd read too much into that kiss. Before he could stop it from happening, Wyatt put everything on the line. "What do you want from me?" Wyatt couldn't help it. He had to know where he stood. Benny had been eating him alive with his stare since they met. That didn't mean anything. If Benny only wanted him as a friend, Wyatt would be okay, but he needed to know that before he lost any more of himself.

Benny's bravery showed itself. He didn't pretend ignorance. "I want you, but I took all those meds on an empty stomach. My head is swimming. I'm hoping I don't puke. It would be nice if I could have a moment with you where I'm not a complete embarrassment. Not to mention, you're hurting and trying to hide it. Right now, I just want to put some heat on my leg while you kick back and think of yourself for once."

Wyatt realized something terrifying in that moment. He could fall in love with this man so fucking easily. "You're not an embarrassment. You're human like everyone else. In fact, I like you more than anyone I've met in a long time." Wyatt turned out to be the one who felt awkward after confessing too much. He glanced around and found the heating pad. After setting it to low and gently placing it over Benny's wounds, he grabbed his phone. "I need to check in with my mom. She's probably still sitting on pins and needles, hoping you liked her food." Wyatt still didn't glance Benny's way as he pushed the coffee table back where it had been, leaving plenty of room to recline the couch. With nothing else left to distract him, Wyatt maneuvered his way beneath Benny's head, letting the man use him as a pillow as he kicked the foot stool out on the couch. He dialed his mom's number. Before he hit the talk button, Benny broke the silence.

"I like you more than anyone I've ever met. Otherwise, I wouldn't care if I threw up on you."

An unexpected chuckle hit Wyatt. He ran his fingers through Benny's hair as he waited for his mom to answer her phone. Benny snagged his hand and brought it to his mouth. He pressed his lips to the center of Wyatt's palm. Wyatt couldn't focus on anything else. There was a strange sensation in his chest. He didn't want to ever move from that spot. Benny moved Wyatt's hand to his chest and held it there as if hugging him. It hit Wyatt. Benny was completely starved for affection. That was something Wyatt could fix. He could and would steal so many touches from Benny that the man would beg for some peace. Wyatt planned to start today.

WYATT'S PHONE BUZZED, snagging his attention. He had no idea how long he'd watched Benny sleep. Wyatt thought he might've dozed off. He'd taken his meds on an empty stomach too. They'd gone to his head. After gently rearranging Benny, Wyatt checked his phone.

Jayden: *I'm off. Are you home?*

Wyatt: *No. Sorry. I forgot about you coming by. I'm staying with Benny for a while.*

Jayden: *You're still with Benny? Why?*

Wyatt: *As I said earlier, he's my friend. He needs help.*

Jayden: *Look, I know you feel some sense of responsibility or something when it comes to him, but don't you think you're going overboard? It's starting to sound like he's taking advantage of your kindness.*

Wyatt: *Actually, I showed up unannounced and I'm refusing to leave. I appreciate your concern. If anyone should know I'm a big boy who can take care of myself, it's you.*

Jayden: *Sorry. I didn't mean to sound like a dick. I just need to talk to you.*

Wyatt: *So call and talk, or type it here.*

Jayden: *Never mind. I guess new friends are more important than old. I'll see you when I see you.*

Wyatt: *Grrrr. I'm trying to be here for you. You're the one who won't just talk.*

Wyatt: *And, I guess we're not talking at all now.*

Wyatt: *Whatever.*

Giving up, Wyatt set his phone aside. He didn't feel like dealing with Jayden's bullshit today. Wyatt was trying his ass off to stay friends with the guy in spite of everything. Maybe it was past time for him to let it go.

CHAPTER FIVE

BENNY: *I PROMISED I'D TELL YOU WHEN I FOUND out about graduation. They're pushing it back to June 23rd and moving it to Freeland Arena. I'll be cleared to put weight on my leg by then but still not cleared to drive, since I'll just be starting physical therapy.*

Wyatt: *I'll drive you.*

Benny: *That's not necessary. I can take a cab.*

Wyatt: *What would be the point since I'm going anyhow?*

Benny: *You're coming to my graduation?*

Wyatt: *Of course. So is mom.*

Benny: *She doesn't have to do that.*

Wyatt: *Don't say that. You'll break her heart. She's already planning a big party for you afterward.*

Benny: *Are you joking?*

Wyatt: *Not at all. There's nothing she loves better*

*than doing mom-type stuff, and she's run out of events
to celebrate for me. You've revived her spoiling spirit.*

Benny: *I'm moved. Truly. I don't have a lot of
people in my life.*

Wyatt: *You do now.*

I don't have a lot of people in my life. Those
words kept floating through Wyatt's mind. He hated
that. Benny shouldn't be alone. Wyatt got that most
of Benny's solitude was self-inflicted, but still. He
couldn't help but notice some of it was due to
awkwardness. Not only did Benny not fit in, he
didn't try. The thing was—occasionally—Benny said
things that gave Wyatt the impression he was lonely.
He fucking hated the man's family had been ripped
apart. Benny didn't talk about it unless pressed, but
Wyatt couldn't imagine.

Other thoughts creeped in, the way they always
did. Waking up with Benny still in his lap had been
damn rough. Benny's injuries made Wyatt scared to
touch him too much. The thought of accidentally
hurting the guy was like getting stabbed repeatedly
in the throat. Wyatt didn't know why he cared so
much, but he did. His concern went way beyond
Benny being the reason Wyatt was still alive. He
cared if Benny was happy, fed, getting around okay,
and... everything. Wyatt just fucking cared.

Wyatt opened his messages again.

Wyatt: *How bored are you?*

Benny: *Not horribly, but I'm a little sick of the same four walls.*

Wyatt: *How about I come get you later and bring you to my house? That way, you're not maneuvering public places yet, but you have four new walls.*

———

HE KNEW AS SOON as he walked through Benny's door to pick him up, something wasn't right. Wyatt ran through their texts in his head. It was so hard to tell tone while reading through the lines. Now that he was here, sitting next to Benny on the couch, there could be no doubt. There was something wrong with Benny. He'd barely smiled all day. Benny's smile was the highlight of Wyatt's day. Wyatt was desperate to bring it back.

"I heard a really bad joke at work today."

Benny didn't bite. He chewed on his bottom lip with his unfocused gaze locked on the wall.

Wyatt tried again. "I got a raise even though it was my first day back." Nothing. "And almost fell down the stairs, because I'd forgotten how steep they are." No reaction. "Two women offered to marry me. At the same time. Even promised to fly me to Vegas," Wyatt tacked on when it became more than clear Benny wasn't listening. He brushed his finger over the top of Benny's hand. "Are you okay?"

The way Benny startled at his touch said a lot about how deep he'd been lost in thought. "Sorry," Benny said, still not smiling. "Did you say something? I guess you're ready to go."

Wyatt's brows drew together. "Talk to me."

Benny's expression remained blank. "What would you like to talk about? Did you say something about Vegas?"

An aggravated growl tried rising in Wyatt's throat. He swallowed it down. "I want you to tell me what's wrong?"

For a second, Benny stared at Wyatt without responding. Wyatt half expected Benny was about to lie and say nothing was wrong. Instead, he shrugged. "Yesterday was my birthday."

"And you didn't say anything," Wyatt snapped. He tried toning it down. "I would've done something for you. Taken you to dinner. Bought you a cake."

Benny waved off Wyatt's words. "I'm not worried over that. It's just another day, but—"

"Just another day," Wyatt repeated, cutting

Benny off. "You're supposed to have cake and presents. And beer," Wyatt tacked on, because he couldn't stop. He'd missed Benny's birthday. It hurt Wyatt's chest—like he'd failed this amazing man in a huge way.

Benny stared at him—emotionless. "It's not important, but my—"

"Not important," Wyatt said, cutting Benny off again. "It's important to me. Maybe I wanted to do something special for your birthday. Did you ever think of that or were you busy being all stingy with your day?"

Benny's mouth finally lifted in one corner. His half smile disappeared as quickly as it appeared. "My mom usually calls on my birthday," Benny said fast, as if he expected to get interrupted again. "It's the only time I hear from her all year," he added with a shrug. "Things over there are different—harder, especially for a woman who fled the country and had a child with an American, only to be sent back. She's not free to talk to me, but she finds a way for my birthday." He twisted his fingers in his lap, breaking Wyatt's heart. "I'm never even sure if she's still alive until I get that call." He shrugged, looking devastated. "I always figured I'd know she was gone the first time the call didn't come." He shrugged again and visibly swallowed. "I guess that was this year."

Benny's devastation was real. Wyatt could hear it and feel it. He had no words. Benny's life was so much harder than he ever let on. The man silently endured. Wyatt pulled him into a hug and held on. Benny clung to his shirt in silence. For a long time, he held Benny against his chest. Neither of them said a word. Wyatt didn't know how to fix this or what Benny needed.

"Tell me what I can do," Wyatt finally said, because the need to help in some way choked him.

"There's nothing anyone can do."

"What can I do for you?" Wyatt clarified. "Do you want to be distracted? Would you like to get drunk? Do you want to wreck some shit? Tell me the first thing that pops into your head."

"All the above," Benny said immediately. "I don't want to think about it anymore."

Wyatt untangled himself from Benny and grabbed his keys off the coffee table. "Let's go, sexy." He helped Benny to his feet. "I know the perfect thing."

WYATT's perfect thing turned out to be something Benny never expected. First, he didn't realize Wyatt had a basement. Second, he never would've guessed Wyatt had turned the place into his own personal shooting range complete with soundproof walls. Third, it was perfect. Benny had never fired a gun. Since he was healing from gunshot wounds, he would've expected being around them would bother him. In fact, once Wyatt covered his ears and taught him how to shoot, Benny found he was pretty good at it. It was also oddly relaxing. Of course, it didn't hurt that Wyatt kept wrapping his arms around Benny, going flush against his back, to help him into position. Benny may or may not have intentionally relaxed his pose just to get Wyatt's arms around him again.

Once they'd wasted a ton of ammo, Wyatt ordered a pizza and unearthed some beer. Three drinks in and Benny found himself telling stories of his childhood and confessing things about himself he'd never told anyone. He liked Wyatt.

"My mom worked at two factories, trying to make ends meet. One, boxing frozen food from seven to three thirty, and another assembling circuit boards from four to ten. I always got to stay up until eleven thirty so we could have an hour together each night. Since I liked having dinner with her, I always ate my meals at odd times. Most kids had sandwiches in their lunch box. I took a box of cereal to school because it was my breakfast time." Benny took a bite of his pizza while mulling over those days. "Of course, now that I think about it, I wasn't old enough to know to fix anything, so it may have just been survival." Benny laughed at his revelation.

Wyatt didn't. "Did no one take care of you while your mom worked?"

Benny shrugged. "I suppose someone did back when I was too young to remember, but otherwise, I don't recall ever having an adult around. It was just me. Maybe that's why I prefer my own company." He thought it over again. "Or maybe I just never had a shot."

"What did you do with all that time alone?"

Since Wyatt seemed truly interested, Benny was honest. "Same things I do now, I suppose. I spent a lot of time online, teaching myself how to do things that catch my interest. Photo editing, website coding, ad targeting; you know, the usual stuff. Then, when I got to high school, all my playing around online had the unexpected side effect of making me really good at learning. I went to Canyondale on a full-ride.

Thank God, or I never would've gotten to go. What about you? You said you played football."

Wyatt nodded. "My high-school team won the championship, and I got picked up by a college in Texas. I went and did my four years before moving on to a pro team in Florida for two years. Honestly, it was a miracle I lasted that long. I was good, but not good enough for pro. It also wasn't the life for me. I made a little money, and I'd gotten my college degree in criminal justice, so I came home and put it to use."

"Do you like what you do?" There was something in Wyatt's voice. Benny had to know.

Wyatt shrugged. "Yes and no. I've bounced from department to department, trying a little of everything. There's a lot of politics in police work and I don't care for that. I'm more of a show-up-and-do-my-job kind of guy. What about you? Do you like what you do?"

Benny had never really thought about it. "I'm kind of lazy, so I guess so." He laughed at his own ridiculousness. "Sometimes I get stir crazy, but I like waking up when I want and working whatever hours I choose. Plus, the way people buy is always changing, so I have to change with it. It's challenging. Yeah, I guess I like it."

At some point while he'd been talking, Wyatt

moved closer until they were hip to hip on the couch. Benny loved Wyatt's eyes, but up close, they were even more amazing. "I know you said it's not important, but if I were to make it special, what would you like for your birthday?"

Benny shrugged. "When is your birthday?"

Wyatt slung his arm over the back of the couch behind Benny, moving closer in his open aggravation. "Nu-uh. It's September third, but you don't get to do that. Even if you never celebrate and never want to, there has to be something you want."

Without thought, Benny's gaze dropped to Wyatt's mouth. Wyatt had used the word "want" and Benny's mind had immediately gone the only place where he craved. He wasn't big on material things. As long as he had a good quality computer to help him escape, he didn't need nice clothes to get him there. But this man, he was a walking talking representation of everything missing from Benny's life. It wasn't as if Benny didn't get chances to meet people. He'd met plenty of guys at school and one or two at coffee shops. Benny had never met a man like Wyatt. He'd also never longed for anyone as much. A hint of bravery rose in Benny. Life was short. He could die tomorrow. His gaze lifted, colliding with Wyatt's. There was so much heat in Wyatt's stare,

Benny knew if he reached over, he'd find Wyatt hard for him. Benny's courage skyrocketed. There wasn't a doubt in his mind Wyatt would do whatever Benny asked. All Benny wanted was a kiss. Just one. He leaned closer. His mouth went dry at the thought of Wyatt's plump bottom lip between his teeth. Wyatt's gaze hooded as Benny inched closer. Benny's heart sped. His cock stirred. Wyatt lowered his head. The doorbell rang, freezing the man an inch from Benny's lips.

"That's for you," Wyatt said, pulling back. Benny blinked at him in confusion. The doorbell rang again and Wyatt stood. He helped Benny to his feet. "The door, it's for you. Go answer it."

"Why would it be for me?"

"For fuck's sake," Wyatt growled, shoving Benny's crutches beneath his arms. "Answer the damn door."

Benny did as told, crossing the room and pulling open the door. Darrel, Richie, Jayden, and Ella were on the other side. Ella held a cake while Darrel had beer and balloons. Richie had four gift bags dangling from his hands. Jayden's hands were shoved in his pockets. Benny's gaze moved from face to face. Shock left him without words.

"Happy birthday," Ella yelled loud enough if

they'd been at Benny's place, his old crotchety neighbor would've called the police. Luckily, Wyatt didn't have any neighbors close enough to hear a thing.

"What?" That was all Benny could drum up.

"Let them in," Wyatt said, his voice heavy with laughter.

Benny automatically hopped backward.

Ella hugged Benny before focusing on Wyatt. "There's more stuff in the car."

Wyatt's gaze moved over Benny's shoulder. "Are Jayden's arms broken?" Even though Wyatt's voice still dripped with humor, his face was tight. Benny's curiosity was piqued.

Ella shrugged. "I have lots of opinions, but I'll keep them to myself. You're all grown men. Get the rest of the stuff out of the car." Without waiting to see if he'd do what she wanted, Ella turned back to Benny. "I have chocolate cake with white icing. Is that okay? I didn't know what you like."

Somehow, Benny's numb lips found a way to work. "Thank you. That's perfect. I think I missed something," he admitted, because his brain still didn't want to work.

Her musical laughter made him smile, even though he didn't know what was going on. "Wyatt called and asked us to help him throw you a surprise party. Of course, if we'd known yesterday was your birthday, we would've done more."

"This is perfect," Benny assured her. He felt like an ass for not acting grateful enough. "You definitely surprised me. Wyatt's been with me all day. I never saw him call."

Wyatt came back through the door carrying several grocery bags. He winked as he passed between them. Benny's hungry gaze followed him without thought.

Ella laughed again, pulling his attention back her way. Her eyes shone bright with humor. "My son can be very sneaky when properly motivated." She closed the front door. "I can see you've got his attention." Her gaze met his once more. "You've also got mine. Wyatt needs someone unshakable. If you hang around long enough, and I think you will, you'll see he's knee deep in shitty people." Her smile reappeared. "Let's take this cake to the kitchen and get the party started. We're already a day behind."

Benny crutched along behind her, heading for the kitchen while trying to process the rapid changes the day had undergone. He'd started out horribly depressed. The ache still sat on his throat, but Wyatt had shown up again right when Benny needed him.

They cleared the kitchen doorway and Benny's gaze automatically sought the man who'd done all this for him. His white t-shirt strained against his muscles. He looked like a freaking miracle to Benny. Wyatt turned his head as if he felt Benny's stare. Their gazes met and held. Wyatt's mouth lifted in one corner. The air thinned, making Benny lightheaded. His knight. The instant that thought floated through his mind, Benny knew. His mom was gone. The day of her deportation, she'd promised him he wouldn't be alone long. She'd sworn a knight would race to his rescue and love him like he deserved. He'd laughed. He wasn't laughing now. She'd done this.

CHAPTER SIX

Wʏᴀᴛᴛ ᴛᴏᴜᴄʜᴇᴅ ʜɪᴍ ᴀ ʟᴏᴛ, sᴏ ᴍᴜᴄʜ sᴏ ᴛʜᴀᴛ Benny questioned his sanity more than once in the past two months. He shouldn't have stopped Wyatt from stroking his dick while he had the chance. Wyatt hadn't tried again and Benny's body screamed for attention, which was stupid, because Wyatt wouldn't stop touching him. He never took a step without Wyatt's hand on the small of his back. If they sat side by side, Wyatt alternated between playing with Benny's fingers and massaging his nape. Sometimes, they'd be doing nothing at all, and Wyatt would pull him into a hug. Not just any hug. They'd touch from shoulder to hip with no air between them. To top things off, Wyatt was always hard for him. Benny lived in a perpetual state of dehydration from his mouth constantly watering.

Unfortunately, everything came back to Wyatt not trying anything sexual again. Not even a kiss. It was maddening. Benny was certain he'd completely fucked things up and lost his chance, but he didn't know how to say that to Wyatt.

Benny searched his mind so intently, he almost missed hearing his name called. His nerves set in. Logically, he knew the place was so packed no one focused on him, but he'd never been more self-conscious. Even though Benny had moved from crutches to a cane, he had to revert to the crutches to make it up the stairs to the stage. He wasn't good with the crutches and the entire get-up of cap and gown made the stairs twice as hard to navigate. The audience erupted into cheers, making Benny drop his gaze. The cheers weren't really for him. They were for what he'd done during the shooting. He didn't deserve the applause. Despite the noise, he could still pick out Wyatt's voice, yelling over everyone. He blushed as he was handed his diploma.

"That's my man," Wyatt screamed, seeming to pick to the exact moment the rest of the room fell silent.

Benny's face was on fire. He hoped he made it through without dying from embarrassment. Surely people could. After all, that saying came from somewhere. Benny's odd train of thought carried him through the trek back to his seat. By the time the ceremony ended, Benny was in hell. His body screamed for mercy and he still had to fight his way out of there while carrying his diploma. Thoughts of Wyatt and where they were headed only managed to distract him so much. Not to mention, the university had given a long tribute for the victims of the shooting. Benny couldn't find a deep enough hole for dealing with that. They'd flashed pictures of everyone taken too soon, and Benny's eyes had refused to focus on the screen. There was no reason for him to have survived other than he'd been right where Wyatt arrived. He'd never thanked Professor Thomalson for that. She'd played a hand in destiny.

He thanked every deity when he spotted Wyatt and Ella waiting for him at the edge of the crowd. Benny nearly collapsed in relief. He didn't know how they could make things better, but he knew Wyatt would try.

Wyatt's gaze moved over his face. Benny knew Wyatt saw his strain. "Mom, will you carry Benny's crutches? He's going to lean on me, so I can help him. There's no real support using those crutches."

"Sure, babe," Ella said, accepting Benny's crutches. Before he could move away, she pulled him into a hug. "I'm so proud of you, and I'm sure your mom is too."

Benny pasted on a smile and tried not to wince. Benny didn't have the heart to tell her his mom was probably gone. He didn't have the heart or the voice. Not to mention, it was a bad time. That didn't stop his throat from swelling at her words. More than once, he'd wondered if his mom had sent these people into his life—like she was out there, watching over him, and sending him exactly who he needed most right when he needed them. He hated the direction of his thoughts. Today, he felt the absence of family in his life more than ever before. He never felt like he could talk to anyone about it. This day would be no different.

"Thank you. It means a lot to me for you to be here," he said instead of making any uncomfortable confessions.

Ella waved off his words. "There's nowhere else I'd rather be."

After turning away, Ella made a path through the crowd. Wyatt's arm encircled Benny's waist. He carried more of Benny's weight than Benny did. "I know you don't want to talk about it, but I know wherever your mom is, she *is* proud. Just as much as I am," Wyatt said for Benny's ears alone. "Of course, that was already true."

"Thank you for this," Benny said, hoping his throat wouldn't swell closed. "I wouldn't have made it here today without you." He meant in more ways than one. Wyatt had been there for him like no one else. Unfortunately, he couldn't think of a single thing to say strong enough to express his feelings. Instead, he went with Wyatt in silence. He made it through dinner, presents, and cake without gazing at Wyatt like a lovesick puppy. At least, he hoped he managed some dignity. Wyatt unbuttoned his collar and sleeves. Dignity fled as he watched Wyatt roll up his sleeves. His attention was locked on Richie and whatever they discussed. Benny couldn't hear a single thing past the sound of his heartbeat. He'd never wanted anyone more. Wyatt was fucking beautiful. Even the way his lips moved caused a flutter in his stomach.

He couldn't stop staring at the sleeves of Wyatt's button-down shirt. Rolled up, they showed off the man's dark skin and muscular forearms. Benny's gaze wouldn't budge. Wyatt laughed at something Richie said. Benny couldn't take it any longer.

"Can I talk to you for a second?" He flashed Richie on apologetic smile.

"Yeah," Wyatt said, looking worried. "I'll catch up with you later," Wyatt said to Richie as he let Benny lead him away.

Benny found the first private spot. Inside Ella's pantry. He closed the door behind them, shutting them inside. The concern written in Wyatt's features almost made Benny feel guilty.

"What's wrong?"

Benny rushed to reassure him. "Nothing. I'm sorry. I just had something I wanted to ask you."

Wyatt's eyebrows rose in question. Benny couldn't make his tongue work. He needed to know if he'd ruined things. Benny lost the courage to ask. No matter how he worded the question in his mind, it sounded dumb. Frustration turned to determination. He was tired of feeling helpless. Benny took a step closer. Wyatt had nowhere to go. Not that he tried. Benny's palms flattened against Wyatt's hard chest. Wyatt's heated expression buoyed his courage.

The door opened. Ella looked as stunned to see them as Benny was at getting caught in her pantry. "Carry on," she said before closing them inside once more.

Horror had Benny dropping his forehead to Wyatt's chest. Wyatt's low chuckle did nothing to squelch his embarrassment. When the man's arms encircled him, the heat in Benny's face was for a different reason. "In for a pound, I guess," Benny said, lifting his head and tugging Wyatt's mouth down to his.

Wyatt didn't react right away. Then, his hold tightened, and Wyatt's teeth sank into his bottom lip. Benny melted inside. When their tongues brushed, Benny forgot his embarrassment. Every time Wyatt had touched him in the past few weeks had led them here. Benny realized now, Wyatt had been waiting for permission.

"I thought you'd decided you didn't want me."

The words so closely mirrored Benny's feelings, he wondered for a second if he'd spoken his thoughts aloud until he realized the confession came from Wyatt. The man barely slowed kissing him to make the admission, saving Benny from saying something idiotic. Wyatt's touch softened. His fingers brushed Benny's jaw as he pulled away.

"Did you really have something to ask me or was this what you were after?"

Benny shrugged. "Honestly? I just broke," Benny admitted with a smile.

Wyatt nodded, as if he understood something even Benny didn't. "I'm glad you did, because I have something to ask... or say—however you want to take it."

"Okay," Benny said, trying to suppress the sudden butterflies in his stomach. If Wyatt had something horrible to tell him, he wished the man would've done it before Benny made a fool of himself and kissed him.

"I'd like to date you. Seriously. I mean, like exclusively," Wyatt said, sounding like he wasn't sure he was being clear.

Benny fought against his smile. "I'd like that too."

A smile exploded across Wyatt's face. "You know we'll have to make the walk of shame from this pantry."

"You're worth it," Benny said, never meaning anything more in his life. Plus, he was used to embarrassing himself. This was just another day, except this time, he wasn't alone. Wyatt made him feel like he'd never be alone again.

IT WAS FUNNY. The room was empty when they stepped out—almost as if his mom had cleared the kitchen so they wouldn't get caught leaving the pantry together. They walked hand in hand and from room to room, searching for the party. It felt damn good to hold Benny's hand in his. He loved openly claiming him. Benny had felt like his since they met. Now, it was true.

They found the party outside. His mom had Darrel trying to start a fire in the metal pit on the patio. "Hey," she said when she spotted them.

"Hey, what's this?" Wyatt asked, claiming the first lounge chair he came to. He'd planned to pull Benny into his lap. His mom grabbed Benny into a hug before he could.

"We're keeping the party going for my boy. I'm just so damn proud."

Wyatt knew without looking Benny was blushing and he couldn't stop smiling. "I am too," Wyatt said, adding his thoughts. "Not everyone makes it this far in life."

Benny flashed him a smile. "I can't lie. I'm surprised I made it. The only Spanish I learned in four years of Spanish class is how to ask if I can go to the bathroom. Between cheating my way through every test and homework assignment, and immediately asking if I could go to the bathroom every time I got called on in class, somehow I managed to bullshit my way through."

"Hey, knowing how to ask if you can go to the bathroom in another language is a good skill to have," Wyatt said in Benny's defense.

Benny nodded, looking serious. "It completely saved my life once on a trip to Cancun after accidentally drinking the water."

Everyone laughed except Jayden. "Why do you do that?" Jayden asked, sounding judgmental as hell. "I'm not trying to be a dick," Jayden added, casting a quick glance Wyatt's way as if he felt Wyatt's ire. "It's just that I noticed at the hospital you do that a lot. I'm genuinely curious why you tell on yourself when something ridiculous happens to you. Why do you draw attention to your flaws?"

Wyatt opened his mouth, ready to blast Jayden.

Benny came to his own rescue. "Nobody really cares if I embarrass myself. If they do, they're not people I want around. Everyone has stupid shit happen to them, and does dumb things, but it's up to the individual to choose how they look at it. Sometimes things are only bad if you let them be. Maybe, instead, it's just a funny story to share." He switched his gaze Wyatt's way. "Tell me something ridiculous about yourself."

Wyatt thought it over. It took him a while. He wasn't used to laughing at himself the way Benny did, but he was determined to prove Benny right. "I always trip over that little step down into your bathroom. It doesn't seem to matter how often I go in there. I trip over it every damn time."

Benny's smile made his confession worthwhile. "See? No one called you an idiot and swore they'd never look at you the same."

"Nope," Wyatt said, proud of his man. "Not that I'd give two shits if they did. Come here; you have to be tired of standing."

Wyatt knew he was right when Benny leaned on his cane more than usual as he moved to Wyatt's side. He patted the spot between his legs before helping Benny sit. Every head, except for his mom's, turned their way when Wyatt pulled Benny back against his chest and wrapped the man in his arms. He didn't bother checking their reactions. The way Wyatt had been acting since meeting Benny, they had to have known this was coming. He'd spent every waking moment with the man since the hospital.

Darrel, being the amazing friend he'd always been, only let the silence go on for half a minute. "Hey, speaking of stupid shit, do you remember that time I thought you'd given me the wrong keys to the new SWAT truck?"

A burst of laughter escaped Wyatt. "You were so pissed off at me."

"Dude, it took me two hours to get out there to the lot to trade out vehicles. It was a hundred and ten degrees out and the keys wouldn't work. There was no air in the old truck and I had to sit out there in the heat and wait for you to make the drive. By the time you got there, I was ready to kill you."

Wyatt couldn't stop laughing at the memory. Benny was right. Laughter was the way to go when you always did stupid shit.

Darrel kept going, obviously feeding off the attention. "Then your ass finally got there, walked right up to a different truck, and unlocked it."

Wyatt swiped at his eyes. He tried talking and laughing at the same time. "Your face, when you realized you'd been trying to unlock the wrong vehicle for two hours, was priceless."

"Two hours," Darrel yelled. "Two fucking hours, I spent in that heat, thinking you'd given me the wrong keys and I'd been at the wrong goddamn truck the whole time."

Benny's laughter made Wyatt's heart smile. Still, Benny tried soothing Darrel's pride. "In your defense, all those SWAT vehicles you use look alike. I probably would've made the same mistake."

Wyatt almost hated to disabuse Benny's defense. "That's true, except Darrel had the VIN and tag number right on the key fob."

"There was that time I spent two hours holding a patient's imaginary friend's hand, so he'd agree to transport," Jayden said, getting in the spirit of things. Wyatt looked his way and winked. He knew Jayden was a good guy. The guy's odd mood aside, Jayden wasn't mean-spirited. Wyatt had known he would come around.

Richie wasn't one to get left behind either. "I remember that. He'd gotten ahold of some laced weed, so I called you in. The funny thing was, it turned out, the drugs had nothing to do with the imaginary friend. Turns out, he was just crazy."

"Yet, you left me with him," Jayden said.

Wyatt listened as everyone tried talking over the top of everyone else, in a bid to have the most embarrassing story. His arms tightened around Benny. Most men would've been offended by Jayden's challenge and the night would've been uncomfortable for everyone. Benny wasn't like anyone else. He looked at the world differently. In turn, everyone around him did too.

While everyone else listened to Richie tell a story about tripping and falling into the bushes,

Benny turned his head and focused on Wyatt. Wyatt's breath caught at the flirtatious glint in his eyes. "You should come home with me tonight," Benny said for Wyatt's ears alone.

"Agreed. By the way you're limping, I'm thinking you need a massage." Wyatt couldn't hide the heat in his tone.

"Are you offering?"

Wyatt smirked. He felt it happen—like his wickedness couldn't be contained. "Anything you want or need—ever—I'm your man."

Benny's mouth lifted in one corner. "Damn right you are."

"What are the two of you whispering about over there?" Despite Jayden's light tone, his eyes told a different story. Wyatt got a bad feeling in his gut.

"About Benny's health. He's still not fully healed, and it's been a long day."

"What about you?" Jayden asked, his voice hardening and deepening Wyatt's fears. "Who's looking out for your health?"

"The boys are looking out for each other," Wyatt's mom said, laughing. "Thank goodness they are, since we've been wearing them out. We should let them go rest while you boys take an old lady out drinking."

"I love this idea," Darrel said, coming to his feet. "It's been a long time since we've seen you do body shots off a stripper."

Wyatt laughed even as he urged Benny to his feet. "I should get Benny home, and Mom definitely deserves a fun night on the town."

Everyone stood.

Jayden shifted forward. "Wyatt, can I—"

Ella snagged Jayden's arm, cutting him off. "What do you say, Jayden? Are you ready to dance with me?"

Seeing his mom's gift of interference for what it was, Wyatt rushed Benny inside without saying goodbye. "I didn't get to tell your mom bye or thank her for putting this together."

"Trust me," Wyatt said, trying to get Benny out of there. "She knows you appreciate her, and she's trying to get us out of here before the guys rope us into going with them."

Wyatt grabbed Benny's gifts and headed for the door. "Besides, I'm ready to be alone with you." He didn't look at Benny as he made the claim. That was why it surprised him when Benny stepped into his path and went chest to chest with him. His gaze shot to Benny's in surprise. The heat in the man's eyes had Wyatt's mind blanking. Benny didn't say anything. It was obvious the move had been all about getting Wyatt's attention. He had it. Wyatt dipped his chin without thought and touched his lips to Benny's. Being with Benny was as natural as breathing. The past couple of months, he'd been fighting fate by not kissing Benny each time his lips had tingled with the desire. Right here was where they were meant to be—in each other's arms. Wyatt wouldn't take advantage of Benny. His respect ran too deep. But he would accept the man's offer to stay the night, and Benny wouldn't go unsatisfied.

Before Wyatt, Benny never thought of himself as a brave person. Now, Wyatt had him reassessing his life. When he thought back on the past few years, Benny realized he'd been nothing but strong, independent, and brave. He'd been alone since his mom's departure and he'd still accomplished a lot. Every goal he'd set for himself, he'd crushed. Even when he'd been nervous or downright scared, Benny hadn't let those feelings stop him. He wouldn't let the shaking in his gut hold him back now either.

As they pulled into the driveway of Benny's

duplex, Benny pressed his hand against his stomach, hoping to stop the fluttering. His bravado fled. He'd invited Wyatt to stay the night in the heat of the moment. Now he was scared he didn't have what it took to please a man like him. Wyatt had played pro football. Not to mention, the man was sexier than most. Benny didn't doubt Wyatt could have any man he chose with the crook of a finger. Benny wasn't that experienced. Sex was embarrassing. What had he been thinking?

"Are you okay?"

Benny dropped his hand to his lap and looked over at Wyatt's question. His nervousness level dipped, became a low thrum in the back of his mind. Lust clouded everything. "I'm nervous." Benny wanted to slap himself. He didn't know why he always said whatever he thought without running it through a filter.

Wyatt's sweet smile made the confession worthwhile. "You shouldn't be. I just want to hold you."

Disappointment slammed into Benny. "Oh."

"And maybe play a little," Wyatt said with a smile so wicked Benny almost came right then. "I still also need to give you your present," Wyatt added.

Since Wyatt had given him a card at the party with a hundred dollars inside, Benny was confused. "You've already given me a present."

Wyatt looked entirely too pleased with himself. "Nope. That was a graduation gift. See, I've been biding my time and watching to see what you're interested in and need before deciding on a belated birthday gift." He reached behind the seat and grabbed a brightly wrapped box. "I'll carry it inside with your other gifts." Benny climbed from the car and followed Wyatt to the door. He eyed the gift box as he dug out his keys. His curiosity was off the charts. He couldn't imagine what Wyatt had decided he needed. Benny felt like a kid on Christmas morning. He didn't get gifts often. In fact, since meeting Wyatt, he had gotten more presents than he had in years. As if Wyatt felt his excitement and wanted to torture him, he didn't hand the box over until Benny gave up and settled on the couch. Wyatt didn't sit as Benny tore off the paper. He hovered, looking unsure of himself. With the first big swipe of paper from the box, a brand name came into sight. It was the most expensive laptop on the market. Benny froze. He couldn't tear his eyes away. No one had ever done anything like this for him before. He didn't know how to react.

"I don't know what to say," he finally admitted. His chest hurt.

From the corner of his eye, Benny saw Wyatt shift nervously. "What's wrong? Do you hate it? You sound like you hate it."

Benny couldn't breathe. People didn't do things like this for people they'd known for three months. "It's amazing." The words came out on a choked whisper.

Wyatt rescued the laptop from Benny's numb fingers. He set it aside before taking a seat on the coffee table. His palms slid up Benny's thighs as he leaned forward between Benny's knees, forcing him to meet Wyatt's stare. "What's wrong?"

Those light green irises that lived in his dreams held Benny's gaze. This man was steady. He was the kind of man that Benny always dreamed he'd marry. Benny had been alone practically his whole life. The words came with no thought from Benny. "I don't know how to lose you, but I always eventually lose everyone. It just hit me how much emptier my life will be once you're gone."

Without a word, Wyatt tugged Benny to his feet and headed for the bedroom. At the edge of the bed, Benny stood still as Wyatt tugged off his clothes, undressing him as if he was a child. "Don't worry,"

Wyatt said in a quiet tone, sounding as stoic as he appeared. "I just want to hold you, but I need your skin against mine," he said as he worked his own shirt over his head. Benny ate the man alive with his gaze. The huge muscles, dark skin, and light scars. Every line, perfection, and flaw belonged to Benny. Wyatt unbuttoned Benny's pants. He kept his gaze locked on his hands. "I could tell you that you won't lose me, but I don't know how to make you believe me." He slid Benny's zipper down and pushed the material down Benny's hips—underwear and all. Once he stood nude, Wyatt stripped out of the rest of his clothes. "All I can do is show you I'm not going anywhere. Get in bed."

With a dry mouth, Benny crawled under the covers. Wyatt had said they wouldn't have sex, but they were nude and Wyatt's sexy body was slipping beneath the covers with him. He didn't know what else to think. Wyatt slid close and rolled Benny to his side where the pressure was on his good leg and his back was against Wyatt's chest. He could feel Wyatt's erection pressed between their bodies, but Wyatt made no move to jump him. Benny's dick leaked. A huge part of him hoped it would happen. He craved not having to make the choice. Wyatt's lips brushed the spot beneath Benny's ear.

Goosebumps coated his skin. Wyatt palmed his hip, massaging. Benny's lips parted on a pant as his eyes fell closed. The man's lips moved lower. His tongue swiped Benny's neck. A moan escaped. Wyatt's fingers dug deeper into Benny's skin. Benny focused on them as they moved closer to his erection. Wyatt rolled his hips as if he couldn't resist humping Benny. His mouth opened wide on Benny's shoulder. He sucked. Benny writhed. A pant slipped out when Wyatt's fingers encircled his cock. He couldn't take it. Touching Wyatt was a must. He reached behind him and palmed Wyatt's dick. The angle was odd, but Benny didn't let that stop him. The way Wyatt handled his cock and the suction of his mouth on Benny's shoulder had Benny ready to fly apart. He moved against Wyatt's palm, seeking relief, even as he massaged Wyatt's erection.

Wyatt's mouth moved back to Benny's ear. His breathing sounded ragged as he tongued the shell. "Damn, Benny. You make me weak. I want to worship you. Feel your cum on my tongue. You're dripping for me." As if proving his point, Wyatt swiped his fingers through Benny's pre-cum. He licked his fingers before encircling Benny's cock once more. It was the hottest thing Benny had ever seen. "You're fucking delicious. Jesus." He openly fucked

Benny's palm as he spoke against his ear. "It won't be tonight, but soon, I'll be inside you. It's killing me to wait, but you're worth it. I can't stop touching myself and wishing it was you. Since we met, you've taken over every fantasy."

Benny moaned as Wyatt set a rhythm that had him on edge.

"That's it, baby. I've had so many orgasms with your name on my lips. You owe me one with my name on yours. One day soon, my dick will stretch this asshole wide and you'll milk me into heaven. Right now, this is all I've got. Let me have it."

The pressure tightening his balls crawled up his shaft. Benny fucked Wyatt's fist, taking what he needed. He ground his back teeth, reaching. His muscles tensed. Benny held his breath. Wyatt's hold tightened. He pumped faster.

"You're so fucking sexy."

Benny flew apart. Wave after wave of pleasure had him gasping for air. Wyatt rolled him to his back and straddled his hips. He kept his weight balanced on his knees, even as his mouth slammed down on Benny's. Their tongues battled. Benny wanted to consume him. Wyatt jacked off between their bodies. His hot cum hit Benny's stomach and chest. Benny's heart swelled. They were real. That conversation in Ella's pantry really happened. Wyatt wanted to be with him. They were more than friends. He could do this whenever he wanted. Benny's head was a mess. He felt too much at one time. Their kiss softened, turning reverent. He rubbed every part of Wyatt's body he could reach—incapable of not touching him. His chest felt too heavy.

"Do you feel that?" Wyatt asked between kisses. "That weight on your chest," he clarified, as if could feel everything Benny did. Wyatt pulled away and pressed his forehead to Benny's. They held each other's stare. "That means you can't lose me, because I feel the same. It's a connection not everyone gets." His gaze softened. "I was meant to meet you, Benjamin Lee," Wyatt whispered, making Benny's eyes sting. He'd never loved anyone more.

AN INCESSANT BUZZING noise woke Wyatt. He tried snuggling closer to Benny and going back to sleep, but it wouldn't stop. Finally, he tossed back the cover and went in search of the sound. He found his phone vibrating across the coffee table, trying to push his keys and change out of the way. Wyatt snatched it up.

"Who the fuck?" He didn't even bother checking the caller ID or his temper before answering. "What?"

"Hey," Jayden said, sounding leery, as he fucking should at three in the morning. "Sorry to call so late."

Wyatt swiped his hand across his face. "Is everything okay?" Because someone better be dead, he silently added.

"Not really, no."

A cool breeze across his ass reminded Wyatt he was nude. He sat on the couch and pulled a throw blanket across his lap. "What's wrong?"

"Since you left the hospital, I've been trying to get you alone so I can talk to you, but there's never time. After taking your mom home tonight, I decided if I ever wanted to have my say, I'd have to just call and do it."

"Okay," Wyatt said, trying to keep up.

Jayden took a deep breath. Wyatt heard it brush the phone. "When I heard you'd been shot and might not make it, I thought my heart would stop. I realized I'd let too many things go unsaid. You know how it is; we always think we have all the time in the world. I still love you."

Wyatt stifled a groan. In his heart, he'd known this was coming. "Don't do this, Jayden."

"I have to," Jayden said, sounding desperate. "That's my point. You could've died, and I would've had to live with knowing I didn't say anything. I just let you get away."

Wyatt pried his back teeth apart. "You let me get away a long time ago. Now I've moved on. I can appreciate you needing to get this off your chest, but I'm dating Benny now."

Jayden scoffed. "It's one thing to be thankful for what he did. He was badass in a tough situation. We all know it, but dating him... really? That's taking gratitude to whole new level."

"That's not what this is about. He's amazing, and why am I explaining myself to you? Look, we didn't work out. I'm sorry you've changed your mind about us, but it's too late. So far, we've managed to stay friends and I don't want to fuck that up. Do you?"

Silence met his question, making Wyatt want to throw his phone. Finally, Jayden cleared his throat. "I don't know if I can watch you be with someone else."

It was like getting punched in the chest. Wyatt wasn't heartless. Jayden was his friend. He didn't want to lose that, but he couldn't be what Jayden needed. "I'm sorry."

"Me too," Jayden said, sounding sad. The click in his ear proved there was nothing left to say. He'd lost a friend.

BENNY CAME awake with a start and reached for Wyatt. The bed was empty. His heart raced into his throat until he heard Wyatt's voice in the living room. After snagging his phone, he checked the time. He'd missed a couple of texts. His brows pulled together. The only person who ever texted him was Wyatt, and no one texted him at one in the morning, which was the time the messages rolled in. He didn't recognize the number.

555-2829: *Wyatt is mine.*

555-2829: *If you don't back off, I'll make you sorry.*

"Whatever," Benny said, tossing the phone aside. People were fucked up. They'd literally decided they were dating less than eight hours ago, and some psycho was already texting him. Benny didn't have time for children and their games. If they found his number, they could find him and say it to his face. Wyatt was his. A smile stretched Benny's lips. Speaking of his sexy man, Benny searched the edge of the bed for his cane before remembering he'd left it in the living room. Instead, he grabbed his underwear. He cursed under his breath as he climbed from the bed, leaning on the bedside table for support. As always, his leg screamed as blood rushed through it. He could feel his heartbeat pounding in his leg as he pulled on his boxer briefs. Benny hopped from furniture to furniture until he made it to the living room.

Wyatt glanced over as he hopped into the room. "Are you okay?"

"I forgot my cane in here," Benny admitted. Even to him, his smile felt shy when Wyatt shot to his feet—nude.

He helped Benny to the couch. "I didn't mean to wake you."

"I don't think it was you. My leg isn't happy anytime I sleep longer than three hours at a time without moving." He nodded toward the phone in Wyatt's hand. "Is everything okay? I thought I heard you talking to someone."

"Yeah," Wyatt said, tossing the phone on the

table. "Jayden called. It seems they just now got my mom home."

"Sounds like she had fun," Benny said, swallowing a chuckle. He could imagine her keeping the guys out all night and rolling in drunk at three. "I'm glad for it. She deserves to cut loose. So do you, for that matter," Benny added.

Wyatt smirked. Benny's mouth went dry. "I had a much better time tonight than any of them. Now that we're up, should we find something on TV?"

"You have the remote," Benny pointed out.

"I'll go find some shorts."

Benny shifted positions, stretching out with his head in Wyatt's lap. "I'd prefer if you didn't."

Wyatt's chin dropped to his chest. The heat in his gaze had Benny biting back a laugh. "If you stay there, you're about to have a hard dick in your face."

Benny rolled to his side, facing Wyatt. "That's not where it'll be," he promised, licking Wyatt's shaft.

"Goddamn," Wyatt breathed, sounding like a man on the edge. Benny didn't plan to move from this spot until Wyatt couldn't formulate words any longer.

CHAPTER SEVEN

555-2829: *WYATT ALWAYS COMES BACK TO ME. You mean nothing.*

Benny: *Who is this? If you're so special, you'd think I would've heard your name.*

555-2829: *Don't play dumb.*

Benny: *Whatever.*

JAYDEN: *I went by your house and you weren't there.*

Wyatt: *I've been staying with Benny.*

Jayden: *Can we talk?*

Wyatt: *I don't think that's a good idea.*

555-2829: *I hear you're still seeing Wyatt. You need to back off.*

    Benny: ***sigh** Get a life.*

Jayden: *I miss you.*

    Wyatt: *Please stop.*

555-2829: *Seriously, you need to back off.*

    Benny: *Seriously, you're pathetic.*

Wyatt: *Darrel wants to go out drinking tonight. Want to be my date? Or should I make an excuse for us?*

    Benny: *I'm up for anything.*

    Wyatt: *I'd love for you to be up for me.*

    Benny: *That too.*

    Wyatt: *Pick you up at 8?*

    Benny: *I'll be ready.*

Wyatt: *Want to stay the night with me?*
Benny: *Yes, I would.*
Wyatt: *Sweet.*

JAKS TAP WAS PACKED and loud. Thankfully, they still snagged a table. It was obvious Darrel had been drinking since long before they arrived by the way he spoke loudly, making himself heard over the crowd. Despite the bodies filling the club, Wyatt only felt one. Benny's cologne filled his nostrils. His warmth pressed against Wyatt's side. It was getting harder to share Benny's company. When he'd picked the man up earlier, Wyatt almost went straight home. He'd run through every excuse he could muster. In the end, he knew he couldn't leave Darrel alone at a bar. That sucked no matter how independent a person was.

Darrel kept trying to tell a story about some guy who hit on him at the mall. All Wyatt could concentrate on was Benny's hand sliding up his thigh. They'd been officially dating for three months, and still Wyatt hadn't tried anything beyond touching. He wanted inside Benny to the point he thought he'd go insane, but something always stopped him. Usually, it was his work schedule. He'd temporarily been moved to nights and had only gone back to days this week. During the short naps they'd taken together, Wyatt had sneaked in some heavy petting, but that was as hot as things had gotten since Benny had blown his mind on the couch. Now Benny had agreed to stay the night. Wyatt wanted to rush him from the bar, or jump the man right there, whatever happened first. He was sick with desire.

Darrel paused mid-sentence in his story. His gaze landed on some point over Wyatt's shoulder. The way his eyes lit let Wyatt know who he'd seen. Only one person ever brightened Darrel from the inside out like that.

Wyatt bit back a groan. It was like everyone he knew wanted what they couldn't have. "I'm gonna grab us a beer." He pressed a quick kiss to Benny's lips, stopping him from searching the crowd behind him, obviously trying to figure out who'd caught Darrel's attention. "I'll be back in a second."

"I'll come with you," Darrel said, sliding out of the booth. "Those first six beers didn't count."

Wyatt smiled when he heard Benny chuckle.

His smile fell halfway to the bar. "I hope you have a way home."

Darrel waved off his words. "You know I can always find someone to take me home." Darrel stumbled, nearly knocking over one of the stools at the bar. "Damn, these things keep getting wider."

Wyatt snorted. "Yeah. That's what's happening." Wyatt pointed at his empty beer bottle and held up two fingers.

"Can I ask you an honest question?" Darrel said, suddenly seeming very sober. "What are you doing with that kid?" he asked, not waiting for permission. "You know how this huge age difference stuff works. He'll get bored and move on in six months."

With every word Darrel spoke, Wyatt's stomach twisted a hair more. It was as if he stole Wyatt's fears and gave them life. That didn't mean Wyatt had to give anyone the satisfaction of admitting it. "I don't know if that's true in this case. Benny is different. He's an old soul trapped in a young body. Anyhow, age doesn't count for shit now. I love him," Wyatt admitted, hitting Darrel with the truth, and leaving the man looking like he'd been slapped. For the first time in history, Wyatt had managed to leave Darrel speechless. Wyatt wanted to laugh. That is, until he realized why Darrel had nothing to add. Jayden stood behind him.

"Can we talk?"

Wyatt's eyes fell closed. Fuck. He hated this. The bartender set two beers on the bar. "Eight dollars."

Wyatt dug his wallet out and handed the dude a ten. "Keep the change." He deliberately took his time. Wyatt had never been more tired of anything in his life than the mess with Jayden. He'd been the first person Wyatt had dated after his divorce. Everything about them had been a mistake, starting with the fact that they saw each other all the time through work. Ending with, Wyatt hadn't been ready for anything serious and there'd been no spark. At least, there hadn't been a spark for Wyatt. It seemed Jayden felt differently. Still, Jayden had been the one who'd dumped him. Wyatt had recognized the problem was probably him being slow to trust again. He'd been willing to stick it out and try to see where things went. Jayden had not. So this bullshit of Jayden missing him was doubly stupid.

Once he'd paid for his drinks, and there was nothing left for Wyatt to focus on, he faced Jayden. "Can it wait?"

Jayden's hard expression said it couldn't before his mouth confirmed Wyatt's thoughts. "No."

Wyatt didn't want this. Everything Jayden could possibly say, Wyatt had already heard. Not to mention, he was there with Benny and no way would he disrespect his man. "Let me put it another way: it'll have to wait until another time. Better yet," Wyatt said, feeling his cool slip. "Let's not do this at all."

The way Jayden ran his tongue over his teeth said a thousand things. Wyatt would regret this. There would be drama. "I'm not a fool. I know you don't want me, but you could hear me out."

"Let's dance," Darrel said, snagging Jayden around the waist and obviously trying to take one for the team.

Jayden's surprise was evident as his gaze slid Darrel's way. "You hate to dance."

Darrel steered him toward the dance floor. "Not as much as you'll hate yourself in the morning if you keep heading down this path," Darrel said his voice fading as he got farther away.

With his cheeks puffed out and blowing out his breath, Wyatt headed for where he'd left Benny. Really, they needed to drink their beers and get the fuck out of there before the shit hit the fan. The instant Benny came into view, all the drama slipped away. Benny's face lit—like he'd waited his whole life to see Wyatt and he couldn't be happier. That shit was more addictive than any drug. Every time, butterflies stirred in his stomach. Without a plan, Wyatt slid into Benny's side of the booth and kept going until he had Benny trapped against the short wall separating the tables from the dance floor. As soon as Benny had nowhere left to go, Wyatt captured the man's lips. He felt more than heard Benny moan. The sound vibrated around their entwined tongues. His earlier confession to Darrel chanted in his head—like it did each time he kissed Benny. He didn't want to scare Benny away with his intensity. Wyatt also worried lust made things seem deeper than they were—like once they slept together, he'd realize the building tension had been all about sex. It didn't feel like it, though. This felt like the real deal. Every time he looked at Benny, thought about Benny, passed a house for sale in good school district, heard a love song on the radio, cooked dinner... the list went on and on. The point was—he had a feeling in his gut every second of every day. That sensation screamed Benny was the one. Even now, he fought the urge to drop to one knee and beg Benny to keep him forever. It didn't matter they hadn't slept together or told each other they loved each other. Wyatt couldn't let him get away. He wanted to stake his claim before someone else gave Benny everything he deserved. Benny was his best friend, and he was under Wyatt's skin. The way Benny's fingers brushed through Wyatt's hair made Wyatt's throat tighten. He'd never been more scared of losing anyone. Wyatt forgot where they were as he committed Benny's every touch to memory.

"Drink your beer," Wyatt demanded before delving back in and stealing Benny's kisses. "Goddamn," he growled against Benny's lips. "I swear I'm trying to stop." Underneath the table, Benny's hand slipped past the hem of Wyatt's shirt. His fingers brushed Wyatt's stomach—skin on skin. Wyatt sucked in a hiss. "Don't forget you've already said you'd come home with me tonight. You can't take it back now."

"I've no intentions of taking it back," Benny said, sounding determined.

Wyatt forced himself to lean away. "Drink your beer so we can go." He pushed his beer Benny's way. "In fact, drink mine too so I can drive."

A chuckle sneaked up on Wyatt as Benny turned the bottle up and chugged. When it was gone, he grabbed Wyatt's and did the same. He set the bottle aside. "Let's go," Benny said, urging Wyatt out of the booth.

Wyatt didn't hesitate taking Benny's hand and heading for the door. He didn't look left or right, nor did he search for his friends. They'd understand. Even though he was in a hurry to get inside Benny, Wyatt automatically timed his steps to compensate for Benny's limp. He wouldn't risk hurting Benny's leg for any reason. At the truck, he helped Benny inside before rushing to jump behind the wheel. His mind was on one thing and one thing only—getting Benny in his bed. He barely got his keys in the ignition before Benny overcame him. On his knees in the passenger seat, leaning over the console, Benny became the aggressor. The man's mouth hit his with enough force their teeth bumped. The lack of lighting Wyatt always cursed any time he parked at Jaks Tap became his best friend when Benny massaged Wyatt's erection through his jeans. Their tongues stroked and retreated. Benny's teeth sank into Wyatt's bottom lip. A moan rose in Wyatt's throat. Benny would push his limits. Wyatt could already feel it.

"Get this truck in gear," Benny breathed against Wyatt's lips. "I need you inside me. I'm tired of fantasizing."

Damn. Wyatt would be lucky if he lasted two strokes. He was so goddamn hot for Benny. "Put your seatbelt on and don't hurt your leg," Wyatt fussed as Benny maneuvered his way back to sitting.

Benny's low chuckle made Wyatt realize he sounded like the man's father. Fuck it. He didn't care. Benny meant the world to him. Wyatt wanted the man safe and healed. He wanted Benny forever. As Wyatt pulled from the parking lot, he realized the truth. No matter what else happened tonight, they needed to talk about what they had. He was insane with the need to grow old with this man.

BENNY SLIPPED off his shoes at the door. He glanced up, meeting Wyatt's gaze as Wyatt did the same. For a moment, the world held its breath. Benny barely saw Wyatt move before his back was against the closed front door. Wyatt was everywhere and more intense than Benny expected. He could barely breathe beneath the onslaught. His jeans loosened. Wyatt's hands were massaging his ass—skin on skin—before Benny had time to accept he was about to get fucked without preamble. There was no backing down. Not that Benny wanted to. Things had just escalated faster than he'd thought possible. One second, Wyatt had looked his way. The next, all Benny could do was cling to the man's shoulders.

Wyatt's short nails scraped Benny's hips as Wyatt pushed at Benny's jeans. "Tell me if I scare you," Wyatt said between kisses.

"I'm not afraid," Benny breathed as he nipped at Wyatt's lips.

Wyatt's lips moved to Benny's jaw, heading south. "You should be. I've never wanted anyone as badly as I want you. You're part of me."

Benny's heart couldn't take hearing those words without seeing Wyatt's gorgeous eyes. He bent and craned his neck, forcing Wyatt's gaze to his. For a moment, the world fell silent as they stared at each other. "You're the one who should be scared. If you do this, you'll be stuck with me, because I'm already sick with love for you. If you don't want to feed this obsession, now is your chance to get out."

The pressure of Wyatt's hands against his back increased. He massaged even as he moved lower. Benny's feet left the ground as Wyatt lifted him from the floor by his ass. Benny automatically held on. Still, Wyatt didn't look away. His expression gave nothing away. Benny wondered if he'd be sick. He'd never told anyone he loved them. "Give me everything," Wyatt demanded on a growl before capturing Benny's lips again. This time was every bit as rough as the last as if Wyatt fought to consume him. Benny's heart soared. Wyatt hadn't returned his words, but neither had he rejected them. That was more than he'd ever had before. More than he'd expected from a man like Wyatt.

A loud knock penetrated Benny's brain. He was so turned on it took him a minute to realize someone banged on Wyatt's front door. They froze—lips clinging. The rapid beat started again.

"Son of a bitch," Wyatt growled, mirroring Benny's thoughts.

"Dude, I know you're home," said a muffled voice through the door.

Wyatt strung an impressive litany of curse words together before releasing a loud sigh. He met Benny's gaze. "I'll take care of this. Why don't you go to bed, and I'll be there in a second."

With a nod, Benny untangled himself from Wyatt's arms and headed for the bedroom. His knees were weak. He could feel Wyatt's heated gaze on his skin with every step. Inside the bedroom, Benny paused just out of sight. He wasn't an idiot. People didn't show up, banging on someone's door in the middle of the night for no reason.

"What do you want, Jayden?" Wyatt said as he opened the door, making Benny realize he'd already known exactly who it was. Benny's curiosity doubled. Wyatt had never seemed unhappy about Jayden coming around. Benny searched his memories for any time he'd seen Wyatt actually speak to Jayden and he came up empty. It seemed like the guy always hung around with Darrel, but he didn't talk much.

"You wouldn't talk to me when I tried at the bar. Now we're alone. You can spare me five minutes and hear me out."

Wyatt sighed loud enough Benny heard it in the bedroom. "Why are you doing this to yourself, Jayden? You're young and sexy. Men throw themselves at you daily. Have you stopped and asked yourself why you keep showing up here and texting?"

Benny's stomach cramped. Wyatt didn't sound interested. In fact, he seemed downright annoyed, but Jayden must think he had some shot or he wouldn't have shown up.

"I know exactly why I'm here, and why I can't stop calling."

"Don't," Wyatt said. Benny's muscles tensed. He fought the urge to storm from the room and find out what Wyatt didn't want Jayden doing. "You know I'm with Benny."

"I know," Jayden said, sounding hurt. "Knowing you're with someone else hasn't stopped me from loving you, so I don't know how to stop trying to win you back."

Well, damn. Benny didn't want to be pissed, since Jayden sounded hurt, but fuck. The dude obviously had no qualms about trying to steal Wyatt from Benny. No doubt, he'd been the one texting Benny nonstop. He fucking hated this. Benny swept the room with his gaze. He should go to bed and let Wyatt handle things. A white t-shirt balled up on the dresser caught Benny's eye. Wyatt had worn it yesterday. Without thought, Benny stripped and grabbed the shirt. As he slipped it over his head, Wyatt's scent overwhelmed him, making his half hard cock stir. He'd been turned on for too long. His leg ached from being on it too much today. Wyatt was his, and Benny was at the end of his patience. The shirt fell mid-thigh on Benny. Benny swiped his hands through his hair, tousling it.

Before he could change his mind, he stepped into

the bedroom's doorway, making his presence known. "Is everything okay?"

Two sets of eyes turned his way. Wyatt's gaze dropped to Benny's toes before sweeping back to his face. He looked ready to fuck.

A muscle in Jayden's jaw ticked. "I didn't realize you were here."

No shit, but Benny wasn't sure that fact would've stopped Jayden anyhow. "It's fine. Are you okay?" Oddly, Benny did care. If he lost Wyatt, it would kill him. He'd probably fight too.

Jayden dipped his chin in a sharp nod. It looked as if he ground his back teeth to a pulp. "You should grab an ice pack for your thigh. It's swelling. You're pushing yourself too hard."

The fucked-up thing was—Benny believed Jayden actually cared. "Yeah. That's where I was headed." Benny took two steps toward the kitchen before pausing and meeting Jayden's gaze once more. He bit his lip, debating. In the end, Benny had to admit he just wasn't that great at keeping his mouth shut. "You know, when you came through the door at Jaks Tap tonight, you should've seen Darrel's face. You're very lucky to have someone who lights up when he sees you like he did. I was almost jealous." Without another word, Benny headed for the kitchen, berating himself. He shouldn't have said anything. He always did this—ruined everything with his inability to keep his opinion to himself.

Benny opened the freezer. Wyatt's arms encircled his waist. Benny's eyes fell closed as Wyatt's lips brushed his nape. Jesus. He hadn't been lying earlier. Benny was sick with love for this man whose touch made him useless. When Wyatt's hands or lips were on Benny's body, he paralyzed Benny. Benny would immediately close his eyes and memorize the moment because life was short. Even if they grew old together, it wouldn't be enough time for Benny's heart.

"I should've stayed out of it."

Wyatt inched the t-shirt up. "Are you wearing anything under this?" Benny's grip tightened on the freezer's handle. "Goddamn," Wyatt breathed when he obviously realized Benny was nude under the shirt. He pried Benny's fingers from the freezer door and led them to the counter's edge. Benny held on for dear life as Wyatt dropped to his knees behind him. His head swam. Benny tried blaming the beers he'd chugged earlier. He'd never been very good at lying to himself. All the blood from his brain had gone to his cock, and Benny might come the second Wyatt touched his dick.

The pressure from Wyatt's palm against the small of Benny's back had him bending over. There was a tiny part of him that had never been more embarrassed over his current position. The rest of him focused on the excitement rushing through him. He'd been impatient for Wyatt for too long. His cock leaked. Benny could feel pre-cum rolling down his length. He was at that stage of horniness that there was nothing he wouldn't agree to do.

Wyatt massaged his ass cheeks.

Benny broke. "Please." Even Benny heard the desperation.

A low, evil-sounding chuckle sounded behind him before Wyatt's teeth sank into his ass cheek. A moan ripped from Benny's throat. Wyatt tongued his asshole. Benny cried out. He was so fucking close to the edge already.

"Wyatt." The plea in his voice was shameless. He didn't know if he wanted to beg Wyatt not to stop, especially since the man's fingers were currently massaging his prostate, or demand Wyatt fuck him hard and stop teasing. Neither of those things passed his lips. Instead, the truth popped out. "I need you."

Wyatt flew to his feet and Benny found himself swept into Wyatt's arms. Benny couldn't stop staring at the muscles flexing in Wyatt's jaw. He looked like a man on a mission. At the edge of the bed, Wyatt sat Benny on his feet and stripped the shirt from Benny's body. Rather than feeling exposed, as Benny would've expected, since he was nude with Wyatt fully clothed, Benny felt sexy. The way Wyatt looked at him was empowering.

"Get moving. I want you ready to get fucked."

Benny scrambled to meet Wyatt's demand. The man's voice and face were hard. It was hot. As he looked on, Wyatt stripped. Benny ate him alive with his stare. He needed to see every inch. Commit it to memory. Wyatt was perfect. His light brown skin and green eyes combination had always had Benny's attention. Now he could add the hard pads of Wyatt's chest and the way his thick cock tapped his cut abs. Benny's already soaked dick dripped on his stomach. Wyatt opened the bedside table. Benny watched as he ripped open a condom and rolled it down his length before coating it with lube. Benny's gaze stayed locked on the way Wyatt's dick moved in his hand. Even as the man set one knee on the bed, climbing on, Benny craned his neck, trying not to lose sight of what he wanted. Wyatt settled between Benny's thighs. His fingers locked on Benny's jaw, forcing Benny to meet his gaze. Wyatt's hold tightened, ensuring

Benny couldn't look away as the head of his thick cock pushed at Benny's asshole. It was intense. Benny fought the urge to close his eyes. Everything about Wyatt was hard and focused. The sweet side of Wyatt was gone. The person who worshipped Benny when they kissed wasn't there. Benny's fingers scratched at the sheet beneath. He held on. Wyatt's gaze never wavered as he pushed inside Benny. This wasn't sex or making love. It was a claiming. Wyatt ensured Benny never lost focus on him. Benny sucked in a deep breath. He didn't have a lot of experience, but this was still unlike anything he'd ever known. Benny wasn't scared, per se. It was more that he recognized the warning in Wyatt's stare. This changed things. Benny was his. It was too late to run.

Wyatt was larger than any man Benny had ever been with. Things weren't going smoothly. In fact, he was downright uncomfortable. Thankfully, Wyatt didn't seem to be in a hurry. Benny kept holding his breath and then releasing it in slow gasps to the point he thought he'd hyperventilate or pass out.

"Relax," Wyatt said, sounding as hard as his stare.

"I can't relax. You're not relaxed," Benny said, sounding as panicked as he felt. Other than the overwhelming sparks flying in every direction, Benny wasn't enjoying himself. In fact, he was on the edge of losing it. It was obvious Wyatt was a very extreme person. In fact, that was one of the reasons he loved Wyatt. Everything about the moment was sexy. That was exactly why Benny was feeling like a failure. The way Wyatt stared at him meant everything. Benny wanted to be sexy and say sexy things. Instead, he couldn't relax or breathe properly. In truth, his thigh screamed from the angle and Wyatt's huge cock was too much.

Benny took another deep breath. It sounded like the gasp of a dying man, deepening Benny's horror. Wyatt's expression changed. He pulled away, making Benny wonder if he'd cry.

"I'm sorry," Benny said out of habit. Fuck. He hated being awkward. The sexy way Wyatt made him feel earlier was gone. Now he was just nude and outmatched. He searched for anything to look at other than Wyatt.

Wyatt shifted positions, giving Benny the room he needed to move his thigh into a more comfortable position. Some of the tension eased from his chest. Then Wyatt kissed him and it eased even more. Wyatt's kiss was always sweet, even when it was searching. When his lips moved against Benny's, Benny forgot his own name.

"You're not ready for this."

Benny's throat swelled at Wyatt's whispered words. No one would ever understand how much he hated himself in that moment. Wyatt was the first person he'd met who made him want to live a life outside the comfort of his home and computer. He was the first person who made him feel normal and like he didn't have to crack jokes to hide behind, so no one would notice how uncomfortable he was in his own skin. Now Wyatt was like everyone else, seeing his shortcomings.

He fought the urge to kick his feet and punch the mattress like a two-year-old child having a fit. Instead, he wilted, withdrawing inside himself. "I'm sorry." He took another ragged breath. "If you don't call me again after this, I get it." Benny's voice broke, making the final words come out in a whisper.

Wyatt's fingers lightly brushed Benny's jaw. The loving caress had Benny in real danger of crying. "Benny." The way Wyatt said his name, as if it tasted like heaven on his tongue, had Benny's stomach tightening in the best way. "I love you."

Benny's gaze shot to Wyatt's so fast he made

himself dizzy. Wyatt meant it. The love was in his eyes. Benny could barely breathe.

"I got carried away," Wyatt continued—like giving a confession. "Being with you, it's everything. The way I feel about you, it's stronger than anything I've ever felt about anyone and I've been married. You make me question if I've really loved anyone else before. This," he said, motioning toward their current predicament. "Is just one more thing to deepen this addiction inside me. I got carried away," he said again, as if this was really all his fault and Benny had done nothing wrong. Benny still didn't believe it, but he could breathe again. He'd also lost the desire to beg Wyatt to take him home. "I forgot about your thigh," Wyatt admitted with a blush that fascinated Benny. "Let's try this," Wyatt said, grabbing one of his huge pillows and shoving it beneath the small of Benny's back. He gently held Benny's thigh. "Are you okay like this?" Benny nodded, incapable of speech. Wyatt led Benny's other leg higher, making room for his huge frame. Before Benny could guess at his intentions, Wyatt slid lower and opened his mouth over Benny's cock. A gasp tore from Benny as Wyatt's hot tongue stroked his length. All of everything was forgotten. If his thigh hurt; hell, if it was still there, Benny couldn't feel it. The suction on his dick was all Benny could focus on. Wyatt held him place, keeping him from hurting himself. It was a good thing because Benny wanted to lift his hips and take his pleasure from Wyatt's mouth. Wyatt didn't take it easy on him. He sucked Benny's dick like a man with a mission. His head bobbed, and he took Benny down his throat with ease. Benny clung to the sheet and reached for everything Wyatt offered. Benny's body tensed. He held his breath. An orgasm tore through him, dragging a moan from his throat.

Wyatt kissed a path up Benny's body. Benny lingered on a high. His mind was fuzzy. His body was limp. All he wanted was to feel Wyatt's lips against his. Wyatt didn't give him time to anticipate his actions. He captured Benny's mouth in a scorching kiss. The flavor of Benny's cum coated his tongue. Before Benny had a chance to tense, Wyatt's dick pushed past the tight ring of muscles surrounding Benny's asshole. Ecstasy stole Benny's breath and fear. Wyatt hit everything at the perfect angle. With Wyatt's tongue in his mouth and the man's cock filling his ass, Benny was closer to heaven than he'd ever been. He was glad Wyatt hadn't given up on him. All his doubts disappeared. Benny could feel Wyatt's barely suppressed desire to fuck him hard. It was in the man's every tensed muscle. Instead, he moved slow, taking his time and kissing Benny sweetly.

"I'll be better eventually," Benny promised, feeling like the worst of failures.

"You're perfect now," Wyatt whispered between kisses. "I wouldn't change anything." Wyatt's lips moved to Benny's jaw and then to his ear. Each harsh breath the man took sounded loud and had Benny panting. Wyatt was back to holding Benny's jaw as he nipped at Benny's ear lobe. His frenzied motions let Benny know how close Wyatt was to the edge. "Benny," Wyatt gasped, making Benny moan at the sound of his name in that perfect tone of desperation. "You make me want a life with you. I want to beg you to give me forever." Benny's mind went blank. His hold automatically tightened on Wyatt with each word he spoke. "Damn, you feel fucking perfect on my dick. Loving you is so goddamn easy."

"Wyatt." Benny heard the pleading in his voice, but even he didn't know what he begged for.

"I'd give you anything, baby," Wyatt said, sounding hoarse.

"I want everything," Benny admitted for the first time in his life. "Come for me. I love you." Benny no longer knew what he said. He just needed to see Wyatt come unglued. The tension was killing him.

Wyatt claimed his mouth. His kiss was rough and deep. It felt as crazed as Wyatt seemed to be. When Wyatt finally exploded, the sounds he made against Benny's mouth had Benny ready to go again. It was the sexiest moment of his life. He'd never felt more powerful. Wyatt's kiss softened. Benny's eyes stung. They felt a lot like forever. Benny prayed he wasn't wrong.

CHAPTER EIGHT_

555-2829: You're crippled. There's no way Wyatt gets to fuck you the way he likes. Not like he fucks me.

───────

Wyatt: *What are you wearing?*

Benny: *Clothes. Do I need to lose them?*

Wyatt: *I was thinking about you this morning in the shower. I'd love to take you against the shower wall with your legs wrapped around my waist.*

Benny: *I probably can't do that, especially since I've been having shooting pains all day.*

Wyatt: *This is sexy talk. Just go with it. Plus, one*

day you'll get better and I'll get to make all this a reality.

Benny: *My pants are off and I'm waiting.*

Wyatt: *I fucking love you.*

555-2829: *You never responded to my last text. Can you honestly say you please him? If not, you should let him go. He's too sexual to be trapped with a cripple. You should be embarrassed.*

555-2828: *You look ridiculous next to someone like Wyatt. He deserves a real man.*

THE BACK of Benny's neck tasted damn good. Wyatt couldn't stop licking it. Benny's laughter didn't help. It seemed like Wyatt hadn't heard it as much lately. Wyatt kept pretending to gnaw on his neck while Benny washed dishes. His heart smiled at the sound of Benny's chuckles filling the kitchen.

"You're not making this easy."

"I know," Wyatt said, dragging his hands down Benny's body. "It's my goal to make you as hard as possible." Benny's laughter transformed into a pained gasp, drawing Wyatt up short. "Damn, baby, are you still have that shooting pain?"

The way Benny's jaw jumped as he ground his back teeth said even more than his nod. "I've got an appointment tomorrow. They seem to be getting worse."

"What time is your appointment?"

Benny didn't answer. His eyes were closed, proving his pain was massive.

Panic hit Wyatt in the chest. "Should I call Jayden?"

"Goddamn," Benny growled through clenched teeth. "That's why he won't let you go, because you call him over every fucking little thing."

Wyatt drew back at the unexpected attack. They never talked about Jayden, but Jayden had backed off, and Benny wasn't one to show an ounce of jealousy. Wyatt was speechless.

Benny shook his head. "I'm sorry. That was the pain talking. My appointment is at ten in the morning."

Wyatt rubbed his back and let it go. He

understood how hurting fucked with everything. "Would you like me to take off and go with you?"

"No. There's no sense in that. I truly am sorry. I don't know what happened there."

Wyatt wrapped Benny in a tight hold and went back to kissing his neck. "Stop apologizing. Tomorrow might be my bad night. Plus, it's my job to make it better. I'm so in love with you. Have I told you that lately?"

"I'm not opposed to hearing it again. Have I told you lately I feel same?"

"Seems like I remember hearing something like that. Can I talk you into leaving this and coming to bed with me?"

"So easily," Benny said, turning off the water, but when he turned toward the room, he leaned heavier on his cane than usual. Wyatt felt like the world's biggest prick for pawing at Benny while he was in so much pain.

Rather than pouncing on him, Wyatt chose to baby his baby. He helped Benny strip and climb into bed. Instead of moving to his side, he rubbed Benny's leg. The humming noises coming from the back of Benny's throat tightened the muscles in Wyatt's stomach. "I'll make you better," Wyatt promised as he leaned over and kissed Benny's thigh, moving higher. Benny's cock stirred. Wyatt bit back an evil smile. He loved pleasing Benny. Wyatt dragged his tongue up Benny's length. Benny buried his hand in Wyatt's hair and hung on.

"Damn, I want you inside me." Benny's breathless tone had Wyatt damn near humping the bed.

"I don't want to hurt you. Let me do this instead." Benny froze. Wyatt felt his body tense. Before Wyatt could react or ask what was wrong, Benny rolled from the bed. He limped for the bathroom.

"I need a shower." He closed the door with a definite snap, leaving no doubt Wyatt wasn't invited.

DARREL: *Want to meet for lunch?*

Wyatt: *Sure. In 30 at the usual spot?*

Darrel: *Save me a seat.*

WYATT: *I miss you.*

No answer came to Wyatt's text. Benny's

doctor's appointment had been an hour and a half ago. He should've been out of there by now, but who knew? Benny had seemed to be out of his funk when Wyatt left for work. He knew Benny was getting aggravated with always being in pain. Wyatt also got that Benny thought he was failing Wyatt in some way. It was total bullshit, of course. Since meeting Benny, Wyatt had been happier than he'd ever been. He was just at a loss as to how to find a middle ground. Tonight, he'd try something new. Wyatt had to take a breath to calm his body before climbing from his cruiser. The last thing he wanted was to meet Darrel with a hard dick. Darrel was the type to take it personally. All Wyatt's erections belonged to Benny.

As he headed for the door of the diner, where he always met Darrel, Wyatt spotted Jayden in the crowd but not Darrel. "Hey. It's a small world."

Jayden smiled. "Not really. Darrel said he'd invited you to join us."

"Us?" Wyatt asked, incapable of hiding his hope. "Does that mean the two of you finally got your shit together?"

A blush touched Jayden's cheeks. "Yeah. You've got a good man. I needed the kick in the ass he gave me last month. No doubt he'll never talk to me again, so I won't get to thank him, but I'm grateful he pointed out my blind spot. He could've easily broken a lamp over my head. Instead, Darrel and I have been seeing each other ever since." Jayden's expression turned serious. "By the way, I'm really sorry. I have no excuse. Hopefully, we can still be friends and you can forgive me someday."

"Shit happens. It's water under the bridge." They made their way inside, automatically moving toward the only empty booth inside the twenty-four-hour diner. Of course, it was dirty. It was no wonder no one had been sitting there. Wyatt stared at the syrup-covered bench. The seat looked like it hadn't been cleaned in years. "That's disgusting."

"Not it," Jayden called before snagging the side of the booth that didn't look like someone had poured an entire bottle of pancake syrup on the seat.

Wyatt shook his head. If he hadn't been in a hurry, he'd go elsewhere. His lunch break wasn't that long. "Scoot your skinny ass over. I'm not standing here like an idiot until someone cleans that up, and everywhere else is full."

Jayden slid over, making room. Sort of. Wyatt was too big and too well armed to comfortably sit next to Jayden. He draped his arm across the back of the bench behind Jayden's head. "I hope they hurry. I like my elbow room when I eat."

"That's because you throw down like you're in a hot-dog-eating... uh oh."

"What?" Wyatt asked, following Jayden's line of sight. Benny sat, turned sideways in a booth nearby. His laptop was open in front of him. It was obvious by the way he sat with his leg stretched out, he was still in pain today. His face was free of all emotion as he snapped the lid closed on his laptop.

"Even objectively speaking, this looks bad," Jayden said, giving credence to his fears that things looked as bad as they did.

While leaning heavily on his cane, Benny slid from the booth. He grabbed his laptop and headed their way. His every step spoke volumes about his anger.

The instant he was within earshot, Wyatt tried explaining. "Benny, we—"

Benny tossed his laptop onto the table and kept walking. "You can give that to him, since the two of you can't seem to stay away from each other." He didn't slow, but Wyatt didn't miss a word.

"I deserved that," Jayden said under his breath.

Wyatt's surprise made him slow to act. He blinked at the laptop he'd given Benny when he'd graduated. Had that just happened? He flew to his feet, banging the table loudly on his way up. Wyatt didn't let it slow him. By the time he made it through the crowded front door, Benny was nowhere to be seen. Cursing heavily under his breath, Wyatt made his way back inside, pulling his phone from his belt as he went. There was a waitress cleaning the empty side of the booth. He dialed Benny's number while she wiped down the seat with a wet washcloth before drying it. When she finished, he dipped his chin at her in a way of thanks as he listened to his call go unanswered. As soon as Wyatt sat, he turned the laptop his way and opened it. He didn't know what he was looking for. All he knew was it wasn't like Benny to make snap judgments. Usually, he stood his ground. Running away wasn't his style.

The call went to voicemail. Wyatt hung up and typed in Benny's password, which he knew because Benny trusted him. His eyes fell closed at the thought. Goddamn it. Jayden was right. This looked so fucking bad.

"Would it help if I called him and explained? I feel horrible."

Wyatt shook his head and focused on the screen. His stomach dropped. The only tab open was one where Benny had been searching for information about his mom. Double fuck. Benny was silently enduring again while he was having lunch with his ex. In truth, he hadn't had time to think about how Benny would feel about him having lunch with Jayden. Everything about the situation was completely innocent, including the moment he'd slid in close and put his arm around Jayden. But, Wyatt realized now, if the shoe was on the other foot, Wyatt would be headed to jail.

"Is there any way you can cut out early and go fix this?"

Wyatt chewed his bottom lip. "I don't know. Someone has to cover my patrol."

Benny materialized beside the table once more. "You know what? Fuck this." He snapped the lid closed on his laptop, nearly taking the tips of Wyatt's fingers with him. "You don't get to steal everything from me," he said, grabbing the computer and starting away.

Benny would've made another clear getaway if Jayden's mind hadn't obviously still been working at one hundred percent. He snagged Benny's wrist before he could get away. "Nope. Sit down," Jayden said, pulling Benny into his side of the booth. "You have to stay and hear Wyatt out."

"It was a misunderstanding," Wyatt said fast

before Benny bolted. "There was syrup all over this side of the booth. We were waiting for the waitress to clean it up."

The heartbreak in Benny's eyes didn't lessen. "Maybe I'll call my ex and we'll have lunch. Enjoy yourselves."

Instant rage hit Wyatt. He'd kill him. Wyatt didn't let it show. "That's not fair, Benny. You know Jayden is my friend, and he regrets everything. Not to mention, he's with Darrel now, and he'll be here any second. We were waiting for him to arrive."

Benny hugged the laptop to his chest, looking like he'd been physically beaten. His gaze finally lifted from where he'd been staring at the table. The dark circles under his eyes made Wyatt wonder how long Benny hadn't been sleeping while he'd been clueless. The shine was gone from his eyes—like Wyatt had killed something inside him.

"I'm not mad," Benny said, sounding more hurt than any one man could contain. "After all, you don't have to worry about hurting him when you touch him. It's not like I can compete with that. You don't have to be ashamed of him. I told you. I always eventually lose everyone." Without a word, Benny stood. This time, he got away before Jayden could stop him.

"What the fuck just happened?" Wyatt asked, sounding every bit as lost as he felt. Yeah, things had looked bad, but they weren't. He never would've imagined Benny not giving him a chance to explain himself. Just like that, he'd lost everything.

———

BENNY STRUGGLED. Everything hurt—mentally and physically. He wanted to smash shit. Benny had never felt weaker. In the past few months, he'd lost more than any one person should. He was tired. Years ago, he could remember his mom telling him a story about an old man who'd killed himself because he couldn't take living in constant pain after a back injury. At the time, he hadn't understood. Now he did. People who didn't get it were blessed. Life hadn't found their line and pushed them over yet. Benny had been well past his line for a while now.

He hadn't stopped pacing since he'd gotten home. At least he still could walk a hole in the floor. Pretty soon, who knew? Benny hated everything. The inside of his mind was black. His doorbell rang and Benny almost didn't answer. Fuck whoever was on the other side. Then he made the mistake of checking the peephole. Jayden stood on the other side. White-hot rage had the doorknob turning beneath his hand.

"You've got a lot of fucking nerve."

"It seems I do," Jayden agreed, looking unnaturally calm for a man stealer. "Can I come in?"

"Sure. Why the fuck not? After all, if you're going to steal every goddamn thing from me, you may as well get to brag." Benny was so fucking mad. He was already plotting where he could hide the body. Jayden had no idea how stupid he was to step foot in Benny's house.

In the center of the living room, Jayden turned and watched Benny close the door. "You should sit," Jayden said, still calmer than he should be.

"It's my fucking house."

Jayden stayed serene. "I know, but you're limping pretty hard."

"Mind your goddamn business," Benny snapped as he headed for the couch. Fuck him. He was only sitting because he hurt.

The moment he settled on the couch. Jayden moved to sit between his knees on the coffee table. Benny ground his back teeth to a pulp. It wasn't fair for Jayden to be gorgeous. He should be as ugly on the outside as he was on the inside so unsuspecting people would see him coming.

"Wyatt didn't know I would be there today. He was meeting Darrel for lunch, and Darrel invited me. I just happened to beat him there. Since he started dating you, Wyatt has barely spoken to me, even though we were friends before you came along. I'm not saying that's not my fault," Jayden said, holding up a hand before Benny could interrupt him. "I'm just saying he's barely spoken to me, much less whatever you have in your head. Do you really think I'd stand for being someone's side ass?"

Benny eyed the man's features and thought about the texts he'd been getting. "No. You'd never give me peace."

Jayden nodded. "I'd be on your doorstep every night, threatening you. But that's not happening, because I was wrong to text or call Wyatt, knowing he was with you. I'm sorry for that. You were right about Darrel. I should've been paying attention."

No matter how hard Benny tried, he couldn't stop wanting to throat punch him. "I got bad news at the doctor today. My mom recently passed away. I've got you texting me to stay away from Wyatt all the time and showing up in the middle of the night, trying to steal him. Of course, then you're all cuddled up with him in a restaurant, so I guess it's working for you. Forgive me if I'm a little underwhelmed by your bid to convince me nothing is going on at the worst possible time in my life."

"I haven't been texting you."

A snort that sounded disbelieving even to Benny slipped out. "Okay. I suppose that's all in my head too. You know I'm not an idiot, right?"

"Seriously. I don't even know your number. Let me see your phone."

Benny was so fucking tired. He passed the phone over because what did it matter any longer? "Whatever."

"You'll have to unlock it," Jayden said, turning the device Benny's way. Benny pressed his finger to the phone and used his fingerprint to unlock it. "Where are these messages?"

Benny pulled them up and Jayden scrolled through them. His face was clear of all emotion. A ringing filled the air as Jayden hit "call" on the number, leaving it on speaker.

A woman answered. "Hello?"

"Kayla?" Jayden asked, sounding accusing. "What the hell are you doing texting Wyatt's man?"

"I'm not," she said, obviously trying to sound innocent without luck.

"Bitch, I just called you from his phone—directly from the messages you sent."

A loud click sounded as she hung up. Jayden growled and called again.

"What?" she snapped when she answered.

"Kayla, don't bother Benny again or I'll have my cousin add that to your restraining order. You need to leave shit alone. Wyatt doesn't want you. Be a woman about it."

Another click filled the air. Jayden shook his head and passed the phone back to Benny. "Just block her. She's too lazy to change her number to get at you. Kayla is harmless. She's just unhappy. I'll take care of her. You won't hear from her again."

Benny accepted the phone. He held on to it a little too tightly. Honestly, he no longer knew if things were getting better or worse. He shouldn't have let those texts get under his skin in the first place, but they'd only confirmed every thought he'd already had. It hadn't been Jayden texting him. He'd been wrong about that, but now it was a second person. "I apologize for accusing you of texting me," Benny said, trying to take the high road.

Jayden shook his head. "Don't apologize. In your shoes, I would've thought the same thing. The thing is, Wyatt really loves you and I can't be the reason that's fucked up. I need to make this right."

Benny's eyes and throat burned. Exhaustion and pain owned him. The day kept caving in on him. He was so damn tired. The last thing he needed was the guilt that built inside him. "He probably doesn't want to talk to me after I showed out today."

"Call him. I guarantee he wants to talk to you."

Benny shook his head. "I can't." His voice broke on the words and Benny had to stop. Why did it have to be Jayden? At the lowest moment of his life, why did it have to be this man staring at him? "I'm sorry," Benny said again. He couldn't seem to stop apologizing. "I've just had a really bad day. Could we do this another time?"

Jayden's expression transformed from determined to worried. He eyed Benny as if trying to put together a puzzle. "You said you got bad news at the doctor today. What did they say?"

Benny's stomach twisted into knots. There it was —the real reason he couldn't tie Wyatt to him for life. He'd never hurt worse. Because whoever had been texting him—Kayla or Jayden—they were right. Wyatt was too good to be stuck with half a man.

Rapid knocking on his front door had Wyatt jogging to answer. He threw open the door, half expecting to find the fire department saying his house was on fire. Instead, he found Jayden, looking grim.

"I need you to come with me," Jayden said as way of greeting.

"What's going on?"

Jayden waved him impatiently out the door. "Get your shoes and keys. We have to go. I was over at Benny's and—"

"You went to Benny's? Damn, Jayden. I told you—"

"Hush," Jayden fussed, cutting him off. "I was over at Benny's, and he was explaining to me how he'd overreacted today, because he'd just gotten bad news at the doctor. He was in the middle of telling me what he'd learned, and he just sort of fell out. He's in the hospital now. We have to go."

Panic slammed into Wyatt. He stamped into the first shoes he saw. Wyatt wasn't one hundred percent sure they matched. He shoved his keys, wallet, and phone in his pockets and was out the door. They were headed in the wrong direction before Wyatt got his bearings. "You're going the wrong way."

Jayden shook his head. "Don't you have a key to his place? He'll need stuff. Remember last time? He didn't have anyone to make his life easier. Now that's your job. Run in and grab him some clothes and whatnot. I'll turn on the lights and get us to the hospital in no time."

Jayden made sense. Benny didn't have anyone else. Wyatt would need to stay calm and make sure he had what he needed. Jesus. He couldn't let the last moments between them be Benny thinking he'd cheated. Wyatt knew how that felt. He'd come home from work early and caught Kayla. It was a shot to the gut. How had he let Benny walk away feeling that way—like the air had gone from the world? If anything happened to Benny, it would kill him.

"Do you know anything about his condition? What did he say they'd said at the doctor?" Wyatt needed info.

Jayden watched the road and shrugged. "He lost consciousness before I learned anything and he never regained it before I got him to the hospital. His vitals weren't great. I don't know. I just got him there and rushed to get you." Jayden pulled into Benny's driveway. "I'll call in and see if they have any info on him while you run in and grab his stuff."

Wyatt nodded and jumped from the ambulance. "Thank you. I'll hurry." His hands shook so hard it took him forever to find the right key. He shoved his way inside, accidentally slamming the door behind him as he went. Benny's neighbor would pitch a fit later. Wyatt headed for the bedroom. He should've asked Jayden if Benny had shoes.

"What are you doing?"

Wyatt skidded to a stop before clearing the bedroom door. His gaze landed on the couch where Benny was stretched out. "You're here."

Benny's hair stood on end. Dark circles marred his eyes. An empty bottle of whiskey sat on the coffee table beside him. "I live here. What about you?" His words were slightly slurred.

"Are you drunk? I've been trying to call you all day. And I thought you were in the hospital. Jayden said you'd fallen out, and he'd taken you in. I was here to get clothes for you."

Benny dropped his head back onto the couch with a snort. "He lied."

Wyatt moved to the front door and looked out. "And he's gone."

"Of course, he is," Benny said, struggling to sit up.

"He said you got bad news at the doctor today. Was that a lie too?"

Benny gave up trying to sit. He let out a humorless laugh and covered his eyes with his arm. "I wish."

The panic that had drained away, at seeing Benny was fine, came back with a vengeance. He moved to sit on the coffee table next to Benny's head. "What did they say?"

"Why does everyone sit on my coffee table? Do you sit on your mom's table?"

Wyatt shrugged even though Benny wasn't looking at him. "Sometimes. What did they say?"

"They said this is it for me. I'll never be better." Benny's voice cracked on the last word, and Wyatt's heart broke for him. "He said there's too much scar tissue. They could go in and remove some to try to ease the constant pain, but I might lose the leg if they try it. So my options are constant pain and a cane, or no leg."

Wyatt wanted to hit something. If Benny would've just let him die, the damage to his leg might not have been as bad. He'd ruined Benny's life.

Benny's throat moved as he visibly swallowed.

He kept his eyes covered as if he couldn't stand looking at Wyatt. "Aren't you glad we're over? All that talk of me healing and you getting to fuck me the way you like; you get to do those things with someone who can."

"We aren't over and fuck that. First off, I'm not with you for the sex. Secondly, there're countless sexual positions. I can find one to work for us. Third, even if I couldn't, it wouldn't fucking matter because I love you." Wyatt was near to roaring each word before he finished.

Benny finally uncovered his eyes. He looked so sexy and broken. "If you think sex doesn't matter, then you've never gone without. When the new wears off with me, you'll just be stuck with a guy who can barely walk and can't please you in bed. Fuck that. I love you too much to stick you with that."

"To hell with this shit," Wyatt said, completely losing his temper. In one swift move, he had Benny thrown over his shoulder and was headed to the bedroom. "You don't get to steal my heart and throw me away. That's what everyone does to me. You're not everyone. You're my person, and I'm not losing you." Benny didn't fight him or run when Wyatt threw him on the bed with enough force he bounced.

Of course he straddled Benny's hips, pinning him in place before he could move. "You want to downgrade me to just someone who cares about sex. We'll do this," Wyatt said, too fucking enraged to calm even a hair. He pulled Benny's clothes off with little to no grace or care. Wyatt had never been angrier with anyone in his life. With Benny nude, Wyatt tore at his own clothes. "I fell in love you immediately—like at first sight. I don't care if people think that's stupid or impossible, because I know it's true. You held my gaze under that truck, so fucking brave. I can remember that moment so clearly because I knew I'd met someone important to my life. You just want to fuck, though. I got that."

A tear fell from the corner of Benny's eye. Wyatt swore he heard it fall—smelled it. That one tear was more powerful than any words ever spoken. Wyatt's anger collapsed in on itself. Then a shuddered breath escaped Benny and Wyatt swore part of him died. He had to see this through. Benny thought he didn't or couldn't please Wyatt as he was. It wasn't true. Wyatt had never been happier in his life, but saying the words meant nothing. Benny needed actions, but anger probably wasn't the way.

Wyatt crawled higher up Benny's body. He opened the bedside table and found the lube. As he fingers encircled the bottle, he captured Benny's lips. Part him expected Benny would turn his head. He didn't. Their lips clung. Then, Benny's mouth opened, and he sucked Wyatt's bottom lip. Wyatt's heart turned over in his chest. Benny wasn't rejecting him. There was still time to convince Benny not to break his heart.

Without watching what he was doing, Wyatt made a mess of the lube. He squirted it everywhere, oiling their cocks and Benny's ass. The mess didn't matter. He needed to make Benny fly. While their tongues brushed, Wyatt rolled to his side. He hated to break their kiss, but he couldn't lie and say he hadn't pictured the best way to get inside Benny without hurting him. On his side. Wyatt shifted positions and draped Benny's knees over his hip. Benny held his stare as Wyatt probed at his ass. Even though Benny's eyes were still bright with tears, his face was dry as Wyatt pushed his way inside. Benny's expression filled with heat. His lips parted and Wyatt nearly came right then. Turned on looked damned hot on Benny. Wyatt went hard and deep. His heart wanted to slow down, make love to Benny. His head said Benny needed to know there was nothing holding them back. Wyatt held tight to Benny's good leg and pounded the man's ass. With his head thrown back and gasping for air, Benny tugged at his cock, openly seeking relief. Wyatt watched the man's dick sawing in and out of his fist. The pressure in his balls screamed for relief. Benny's tight ass felt like heaven on his cock. Wyatt needed Benny's orgasm. He changed angles, ensuring his thrusts hit Benny just right. A cry tore through the room as jets of cum coated Benny's body. His ass tightened on Wyatt's dick, threatening to break him. Pleasure slammed into Wyatt, stealing his breath. He clung to Benny and rode every wave.

"Holy shit, Benny. I love you so goddamn much. You can't leave me. It would kill me. Promise me you won't leave me." Wyatt didn't care if he sounded desperate. Without Benny, his life would be less than ever before. It would be meaningless.

Benny stroked his arm. "I'm not going anywhere. You're the love of my life. I'm sorry I scared you."

Uncaring of the mess and still suffering aftershocks, Wyatt straddled Benny's hips again and kissed him deep. They needed to talk about where they were headed. Wyatt couldn't live with the constant fear of losing Benny. But right this second, they just needed to be. He'd come closer to losing Benny than he could live with.

For hours, Wyatt watched Benny slip in and out

of sleep. He was beautiful. It was no chore, but his mind wouldn't quiet. Benny needed help. He needed Wyatt to be more than a guy who stayed the night and helped him from the bed to the couch and back again. Wyatt needed to think. He had to come up with a plan. After slipping from the bed, he headed for the bathroom. He flipped on the light and immediately tripped down the step.

"Who the fuck designed this shit?" Wyatt grumbled under his breath.

A low rumble of laughter drifted from the bed. Wyatt's gaze shot that way, finding Benny watching him. "I fucking love you."

A smile lit from Wyatt's chest and tugged at his lips at Benny's claim. "I love you too. Go back to sleep." When Benny closed his eyes, Wyatt shut the door. He needed to get moving and coffee. Lots of coffee. He turned on the water and splashed his face. As he cupped more running water in his hands, Wyatt froze and stared at the stream through sightless eyes. He knew what needed to be done. It was well past time he acted. He'd let Benny sleep. In the morning, Wyatt intended to take over the man's life.

The sensation of someone staring at him dragged Benny from his dreams. Wyatt leaned against the headboard, fully dressed and watching him.

"Good. You're awake."

Benny blinked, trying to get his bearings. "Have you been awake long?"

"All night," Wyatt said, sounding over caffeinated. "I've been up researching, and I've made some decisions."

"Okay," Benny said, speaking through a horrible case of cotton mouth.

"First, once you're up, showered and dressed, we're going to get married."

Benny blinked some more. "Was that a proposal?"

Wyatt's eyebrows rose. "No. It was a demand. You've had the meat. Now you're buying the bull. I expect to be made an honest man."

Benny rolled to his side and tried harder to keep up. He searched his brain and came up empty. There wasn't a single argument he could make. If Wyatt wanted to get married, what could Benny say?

He deserved that much, and Benny loved him. "Okay. Anything else?"

Wyatt's smile looked triumphant. "I've decided I'm taking over your life. You see, you don't think enough about yourself or your health. That's where I come in. After we get back from two days in Vegas, which I've already booked, we'll go see your surgeon and we'll talk this out. You can't live the rest of your life in pain."

"I see," Benny said for lack of anything else. "And I have no say in this?"

Wyatt nodded. "Exactly. See, the way I see it is— you've been alone too long. You need help and don't know how to ask, so I'm taking your choices away. I love you and won't let anything bad happen to you. You can trust me to be your strength while you deal with everything."

Benny felt lighter just listening to Wyatt talk. He was tired and too scared to make any decisions. There was no one else he trusted. His eyes burned, because Wyatt was too amazing, and he needed him. It hurt his throat to voice his deepest fears. "What if I lose the leg?"

"Baby, I won't let you deal with anything alone. I plan to be everything for you until the very end. You won't have time to carry any of the fear or worry because I'm doing it for you. It's my turn to carry you. Let me do it."

"I love you." Even though the words sounded strong in his head, they barely reached a whisper in reality.

Wyatt's smile tugged at his heart. In one look, Benny knew hearing those words meant everything to Wyatt, and he was the luckiest bastard alive to have Wyatt in his life. "I love you too. Get up. We're getting married today."

A burst of happiness sent Benny scrambling for the shower. He couldn't wait to have everything he never knew he wanted.

CHAPTER 9

Six months later...

"Raise your glasses. I'm making a toast." Everyone followed Darrel's lead and raised their glasses. "Benny, you're another year older."

"And wiser," Richie added.

"And getting sexier every day," Wyatt said, throwing in his two cents.

Darrel huffed. "I'm making the toast here." He straightened his shoulders and lifted his beer once more. "When you blow out your candles, I don't know what you'll wish for, because you have it all, you lucky bastard. However, I still hope you find even more of the happiness that's eluded me." Darrel's toast said a lot. Benny had been wondering why he hadn't seen Jayden around in a while. Maybe it was time for him to interfere.

"Awww," Ella cooed. "Maybe I should let you blow out the candles instead of Benny."

Benny stared at his husband as the others traded jibes. He was still in his uniform, having barely made it home in time for Benny's birthday party—thanks to a standoff at a local hotel. Wyatt mouthed "I love you" and Benny's smile wouldn't abate. Darrel was right. He was the luckiest man alive.

As he watched Ella light the candles on his cake, he realized Darrel was right about something else— he had no idea what to wish for. The last year of his life had been insane. He'd been shot. Met the man of his dreams. He'd lost his mother. It was official. He'd gotten a letter from an elderly aunt he hadn't known existed three months ago. His mom had lived a hard life and died young. At least he knew she was at peace now. Benny had also fallen in love and gotten married. He'd endured several surgeries. His limp was worse now, but he'd kept his leg and was relatively pain free. That was all he could ask for.

Tendrils of smoke swirled through air as Benny blew out his candles.

Wyatt's lips touched his ear. "What did you wish for?"

A smile pulled at the corners of Benny's mouth. "I can't tell you or it won't come true."

"That's not how we work," Wyatt said, running his hand up Benny's inner thigh beneath the table. "You tell me what you want and I set it at your feet."

It was true. That was how they worked. "I wished for at least sixty years with you."

"Done," Wyatt said, as if it was that easy.

Maybe it was. After all, they were meant to be. Never had fate been so blatant in a pairing as with them. They'd already almost died together. Living together would be a snap, and it was.

Charity Parkerson is an award winning and multi-published author with several companies. Born with no filter from her brain to her mouth, she decided to take this odd quirk and insert it in her characters.

*2015 Readers' Favorite Award Winner

    *Winner of 2, 2014 Readers' Favorite Awards

    *2015 Passionate Plume Award Finalist

    *2013 Readers' Favorite Award Winner

    *2013 Reviewers' Choice Award Winner

    *2012 ARRA Finalist for Favorite Paranormal Romance

    *Five-time winner of The Mistress of the Darkpath

Connect with her online:

--Join my street team: facebook.com/TeamCharityParkerson

--Sign up for my newsletter: http://bit.ly/CharityNews

--Website: charityparkerson.com

--Facebook: facebook.com/authorCharityParkerson

facebook.com/TheMenofSin

--Twitter: twitter.com/CharityParkerso

admin@charityparkerson.com

www.ingramcontent.com/pod-product-compliance
Lightning Source LLC
Chambersburg PA
CBHW071134200626
46817CB00018B/2949